A Persona

MW00886677

Before diving into the beginnings of the story, I wanted to lay out my intentions in writing this piece. First, I'm going to explain what writing is to me. Not just as a task as with class-assigned essays, but what it does for me.

Writing had always managed to be a way of expressing my thoughts, a way to let out what I had been feeling for the day, without having to hold back. Of course, it is no secret that there are implications for immoral pieces, but the simple truth of one's psyche can be puzzling even when written in the simplest terms. For example, I write, *the clock thunderously struck forward as midnight approached, each second an eternity, and each tick an eruption*, and one automatically pictures the "clock" to be rather large. Really, the situation surrounding the importance of the clock, in context, could paint the timepiece to be either insignificant or colossally important— it's up to the reader's interpretation.

This is the grandness of writing, its ambiguity, mystery, and complexity. I've typically thought of myself to be a rather creative individual, always drawing or thinking or inventing or writing. Eventually, I picked up philosophical writing in my spare time. Along with lyrics to random songs I'd jot down was the basic outline to the story I am about to tell.

I figure it's probably the best way to let go of the boundaries often placed on my creativity. These metaphorical shackles that imprison my illogical reasoning, I believe, are tightened at some points, furthering my need to express without limits. The most blatant example is in multiple choice exams, particularly in regards to passages. My goodness, they irritate me.

What I mean is this: why are there multiple choice questions based on reading a passage and interpreting it "correctly"? What great literary work ever had a single interpretation or was written with only one point of view? Did Fitzgerald write *The Great Gatsby* with only one theme? Did Stowe write *Uncle Tom's Cabin* expecting only one reaction? What is good writing with concrete goals of the author? There cannot be one answer to a question regarding literary intentions, it's ridiculous to expect such hollow art. If my methods were considered, reading would be removed from all standardized tests and exams, let the student write and support their interpretations, don't guide them and direct their understanding of literature to how an official sees best. But then again, I'm only seventeen years of age, what is my opinion worth?

Truly, I've always thought of myself as a rather complicated person. Sometimes, my mind works against itself and I'll doubt my abilities, or I'll use my imaginative method of thinking too much and it will end up retarding my progress. Often times, I'm very wordy with my expression. I just prefer elegance in my works as opposed to bland, contemporary, generic vernacular. Maybe it's annoying, but at the end of the day, it's part of what makes me who I am. That being said, if I can offer a word of advice to anyone reading this, regardless of how old you are, don't EVER let someone change who you are. I've gone through bits of my life in the past where I tried morphing my character to fit someone else's desires, and I wistfully imagine those moments to be different. Who cares if you aren't the most popular kid? Or if people make fun of you for who you are? Be you. If you don't know what being you is, then find you. It's never too late to discover who you really are.

I contemplated indulging in some of my true passions intensely while writing this, but decided against it, for hopes to keep clarity with regards to the story. An example being my longing for bilinguality in English and Spanish, I kept confined to this introduction, as I felt the use of other languages in the story may provide too much confusion. Another being my love for running, though on and off sometimes, I kept to only one segment. Overall, the only off-topic sections in this book are really seen in philosophical discussions, where I make the effort to express my thoughts.

Anyway, it should be expected, rather obviously, that this piece is not a simple exemplification of a generic story. Nor is it meant to have one truth underlying in the theme. It is meant to be debated and misunderstood — as all great works are. Not everything in this story replicates beliefs of mine, though some are still worthy of discussion. I tried my best to blend things as well as I could, weaving in and out of monologue. Please keep in mind, I've never written something of this length or complexity. Enjoy, a fictional rendition of my conscious train of thought.

— *San Francisco, California* —

Prologue ~2010

High school has been good to me. I kinda wish there were some challenge to it, though. Last year I signed up for the hardest schedule they could give me, but it really hasn't given me that much trouble. Anyways, that's not important. I've got a party tonight, I ought to get ready for it. I gotta pick up a few of my buddies on the way there. Haven't seen Jimmy in ages!

Apparently, the house we're rocking at has a huge pool in the backyard, I'm a bit excited for that. It's already 8:00 pm, no use in waiting around at home any longer. I'll swing by the few houses I've gotta hit, and then speed over there. I'm lucky I haven't gotten pulled over with how fast I go. I've gotta be careful. *Nah.*

The party was popping as soon as I stepped foot inside the house. It was filled with people not just from my school but from schools all over the area. I knew everyone from my junior class, of course, but it was a lot more than just my junior class. We headed outside for the pool, me and my guys, and it wasn't as occupied as

I'd expected. Ninety degrees this late at night? What heat wave rolled in to San Francisco?

Music was blaring from the speaker a couple of rooms away from the back screen doors and the trail of sound carried its way out to the few of us still chilling in the pool at 10:00. Alyssa and I were coupled together by the stairs with some other groups on the other sides. I'm feeling a bit upbeat tonight, so I'm sticking by her for the night. I drove here so I gotta make sure I don't get too wasted, being that I'm my own ride. *And probably Alyssa's.*

The night died down at around 2:00 am, honestly a bit earlier than I had expected for such a grand party. And when I say grand, I mean grand. The staircase was drenched in crushed beer cans and dead tips of cigarettes. Empty cardboard boxes flooded the kitchen and dining room with the marijuana aroma entranced the halls. A few glasses were smashed on the ground, but not too many. Cars piled up down the block from people eager to get close to the house. I enjoyed the rush of people here and there, but I cared more for the relaxed celebration going on outside of it all.

Alyssa and I snuck out of the crowd and jogged off to my car, stumbling around the street a little bit. I offered to take her home for the night, I knew a way to get into my house undetected. She texted her parents saying she'd spend the night at another one of her friend's houses. Not believable at all, but it was already two in the morning, what more harm could be done.

I woke up with her already awake and a bit panicky, fumbling with her shirt on the ground. I tried to comfort her, which was a bit weird for me. Usually, I just drove the girl home. She was furious at me for "taking advantage of her", when I really don't know what she's talking about. She stormed out of the room and demanded that I take her home, and I followed, casually. I grabbed a cherry Pepsi from the fridge on my way out, and cracked it open as soon as I stepped outside. It was hot.

"Let's go, what are you waiting for?" she screamed at me, stomping outside of the passenger door of my car. I didn't change pace at all. She gave me the directions to her house which was only about three minutes away. Probably a fifteen minute walk if she had to. Maybe even ten.

As the car came to a stop, I reached my hand out for her, to tell her goodbye now that I had been woken up with the unhealthy amount of sugar in the drink, but she just simply slammed it in my face. I guess I deserved it, for the whole last night situation, but I was just having a little fun. I've never had a girl give a sincere goodbye to me, like a really heartwarming farewell. It's always fake. *I wonder what it would feel like.*

Maybe I'll change. Maybe this isn't who I'm meant to be. I've been doing this for so long, it's just been engraved into my mind as my behavior, but, maybe I can change. Will I enjoy myself more? I'll find out, I guess.

Isolation, Hospitality

The blood was still fresh when my squad and I arrived the scene. The smell crept through our open windows before we could get out of the car, it seemed as if the worst was true. She was dead. Lifeless. From down the block her body was visible, and not a muscle had moved since it was introduced to our vision. I parked the car on the curb and rushed to the scene, my partner following close behind. As we stood over her still body, we inspected the area for evidence, anything that could give us a lead. The pool of blood next to the incision on her stomach was still shining in the light, implying that the murder had been committed no longer than in the previous hour. We scanned the street for any alleyway or corridor, anything that could point us to where the killer may have snuck off, even scanning the ground for footprints or ditched weaponry. The search, however, was to no avail.

"Well, this sucks," Ellis observed cynically. Years of work as a detective had impressed a rather dark but justified view of crime in his mind. This was just another situation that emphasized that impression.

"No, really? You find anything?" I responded, equally dismal.

"Nada."

We walked around the scene a while longer as the lights atop the cars glowed in the darkness of the night. Aside from our presence, the street was empty- the perfect conditions for an unseen crime on a defenseless woman, especially a younger woman, such as the one who now lay beneath the starched white sheet. We made our final observations and concluded there was not much for us here. The scene was clean, aside from her body. This criminal was seemingly careful, and knew it was better to dispose of the knife outside of this vicinity.

"Hopefully analysis crew picks something up from the lot, there was nothing to find there. Simply a slash and dash. Killed her and booked," Ellis said as we piled back into my car and drove off toward the station. It had been a long day, and this just put the cherry on top.

"Presumably. There's nothing here. CSI should turn up something. This night just needs to end." I said back, barely mustering up the energy to speak. Multitasking had been reduced to the occasional word or two and driving, exhaustion had consumed me. After twenty minutes of boring, drawn-out driving, we reached the station. Immediately, I grabbed my things out of my locker and headed towards my car, said my goodnights to everyone, and proceeded for home. Eleven hours felt like an eternity.

When I got home, which I speculated, took another lengthy drive, I threw my coat on the chair in the entrance and hopped on to my bed, in uniform. It had not been more than five minutes, and I dozed off.

Ring. Ring. I awoke to the blaring siren of my alarm clock two feet away from me. Another day. It was a sluggish morning, unfortunately, even with the pleasant amount of sleep overnight, I still found difficulty in my usual routine. After about three minutes, I finally realized I was still in uniform, and that put me back on track. I rushed out of the house, sloppily locked the door as I fumbled with the keys, and drove off for the Starbucks down the street. This is really the life of a twenty-four year old detective from San Fransisco, I guess.

The line in the cafe was shorter than usual this time. Typically, there's a pretty long wait for coffee at six thirty in the morning. While waiting in line, the lady in front of me struck up conversation with me, and I felt inclined to carry it on as more than small talk.

"Detective, huh? Admirable," she said, flashing a subtle grin as she eyed my badge.

"Indeed. How about yourself?" I responded, half interested. As she began to inform me, I stared at the menu, as if I didn't already have my order memorized. Tall caramel macchiato with whip, grande if I'm extra tired. This may be one of those days.

"Accountant," she said, maintaining that gentle smile.

"I'm Theodore, or Ted, whichever you prefer."

"Theodore," she paused, "Alice," smiling with a charm for the third time.

"Nice to meet you, you're up," I said, smiling back at her and pointing at the clerk. Our conversation had distracted her as the line advanced. Her lips formulated the common response of *nice to meet you too*, but her realization that she was next in line halted those words from escaping her mouth. We made our orders, and I decided to match her's of peppermint mocha, to be different for a day. Exiting the building together, I proceeded toward my car. She followed, leading me to assume that she walked to work.

"You need a ride?" I asked her, I felt obligated.

"If you insist," she replied, giggling timidly. She guided me to her building, which was only about three blocks from the coffee shop, and I pulled over to the curb. Before she stepped out of my car, she handed me her phone, already open to the 'new contact' screen, "We should talk again sometime."

"We should," I said back, with a sliver of nerve arising throughout my body as I put my number into her phone, and handed it back to her.

"Goodbye for now, Theodore," she cheered with the same, thought-provoking smile emerging for a fourth time. She galloped away toward her building and as the door shut and I watched her through the car window, I couldn't help but smile in a similar manner. It had been a while since I'd smiled like this. *Girls have a tendency to make you do that, I guess.*

The ride to the station was rather energetic, as I pumped up the volume on my radio, rolled the windows down, and enjoyed the refreshing breeze that circulated through my car in the seventy-four degree weather. It was almost fitting, as 2Pac's "California Love" started playing, and I turned the volume up a little louder, in agreement with his affection for the state. By the time I arrived at the station, I had forgotten I wasn't still in high school. It sure felt like it.

"Morning, Ted. Forensics came back with an identification on the victim, Victoria Parker, twenty-four years of age. She had been walking down the street on her way home from work, dark alley is a perfect hiding spot, the killer jumped in front of her, wrestled with her a bit but not much. Parker was basically defenseless, stabbed and dying before she even knew what was happening. No sign of anything that points us to a perp," Ellis informed me immediately as I stepped foot inside the building, not even giving me a chance to collect my thoughts in preparation for another work day. I was still in the music!

"Right, okay. Okay. Occupation?" I replied back, trying to piece things together.

"Worked in US Bank, downtown. Employed about two years ago. Shall we?"

"Probably. Let's go." I instructed Ellis, and we hopped back in my car. I was trying to figure out anything on this, but the murder scene was left essentially spotless. Nothing to give us a lead. *There's always a lead, somewhere, Teddy, you just have to find it.* I kept thinking, and nothing was coming to mind. We pulled up outside the US bank building, and rode the elevator up to the floor she worked on. We met with the lady who seemed to be the bank manager, as her office was central on the floor.

"I assume you're here to ask questions about Miss Parker," she prompted. Her voice was fragile, but prepared.

"Yes, I'm Ted, this is my partner, Ellis, and we're detectives for the San Francisco Police Department," I explained, as I gestured to Ellis, and we sat down after shaking hands.

"Caroline."

"It's a pleasure. I would rather not waste more of your time, I know this must be difficult. Was Victoria an outspoken woman in the workplace?" I inquired, trying to at least come off as gentle.

"Hardly. She usually just kept to herself and got her work done. I was so shocked when I heard about her death. She was the most innocent girl. There was nothing about her I could see that may have caused this. At least, not from here."

"Anyone that may have had a problem with her?"

"I don't think so. I'm telling you, she mostly kept to herself. No one really knew her that well."

"Okay. That's really unfortunate, if you hear or see anything new, give me a call," I said to her grimly, as I handed her my card. This encounter got us nowhere. We exited the building the same way we entered and regrouped in the car.

"That was pointless," Ellis said, reading my mind.

"Okay. Work was a no-go. Where to next? Family?" I questioned.

"Probably. I'll give Amber a call at the station, see if she had any family here," Ellis responded, expertly. He called up Amber and apparently the woman had family in Oakland, so we left for it. It was nice to cross the bridge again, though, it had been a while since I was in Oakland. The bay area is so nice, the waves brushing up against the supporting pillars sparked memories of the past. I made sure to take in the view of the cities, breathing in the culture.

We arrived at the victim's family's house after about twenty-five minutes of driving, turns out it's her parents'. In speaking with her family, we continued to have little success. More of the same. Her mother told us that she had been relatively quiet since her younger days in high school, kind of just focusing on bettering her own life. Our meeting was quickly interrupted by an unexpected phone call from the station.

"Right outside the US Bank building, another murder. This time, a body seems to have been dropped from above. Get there fast, maybe we can catch the killer," from Amber. We grabbed our things, apologized to the family, and booked it back to San Fran.

"We gotta catch this jag," I told Ellis as he was speeding down the bridge at sixty miles per hour. He whipped around the corners once we got back to San Francisco, sirens blaring and our surroundings a blur. We pulled up to the spot of the crime, where other squad cars were already stationed. I motioned for Ellis to keep driving and yelled for him to go ahead. We swung around the back of the building across from it, California 101. We hopped out and darted into the building.

"How did you know this was the building?" Ellis questioned as we raced inside.

"Body positioning. It was farther away from this one. If someone is pushed off the building, they would go farther. If it's suicide, probable that it's closer to the building they jumped off of." I took the stairs in the Southeast sector, while Ellis proceeded toward the Northern side. I withdrew my pistol from my side, and slowly repeated the same, precautionary steps as I ascended. *Aim. Check. Elevate. Aim. Check. Elevate.* Each floor rose the nerve in my mind. The hairs along my neck, though ever so finite, stood straighter.

It was the crash, perhaps, that startled my judgment. Without realizing, I had backed into a canister at the edge of the stairs, which was sent into a tumble by the extension of my leg. Focus had been lost, seconds, which were as valuable as days, had been lost. I quickly shifted into a defensive stance, in case the criminal had been in the stairwell and heard my accident. Floor after floor, I grew increasingly doubtful that they had still been here. Eventually, I rose to the top floor where I met up with Ellis. Both of us had been unsuccessful.

"Nothing. Not in my staircase, you either?" he said, slightly out of breath.

"Nothing. Damn it! Where could he have gone? I don't get it," I said, in clear frustration. Tension was building up inside me, I despise my own failure. This man needs to be caught, whoever he is.

We must first identify him, though. I examined the top of the building, hoping for anything that would give us a sign of where the killer had gone, or who they might be.

"Search that side," Ellis barked, pointing toward the ledge that the victim was pushed off of.

My instincts told me that the victim had been forced up here. I looked around, and found only a syringe, used most likely to knock the victim out while the murderer kidnapped him. This was infuriating. Every death, every victim and their families, each of them are of my own responsibility. My own failure. I can, with certainty, predict I am going to be up late, I need to solve this. If I care about something, it favors to cloud my interest. I'm focused now. Tunnel vision.

We rolled back up on the station after a few more hours of surveying the area and building and interviewing some of the employees of the building. We eventually found the security patrol and their headquarters and scanned the footage of the building over the past twelve hours. There was really nothing suspicious, this killer has to know the building well. They've got to know where the cameras are and aren't, and how to avoid being caught. There was little to no evidence to be traced back to the perpetrator in the building as a whole, which proved to be that much more convincing of the killer's capability. An intelligent, talented criminal requires a detection team of equal intellect. It's time I take control. I need to step up for this agency and lead it in the right direction, owning up to where we take the wrong turns as well. I ordered, firstly, for thorough background checks on both of the victims.

"There's a big similarity between the two: same high school. Joseph Walker and Victoria Parker," Amber informed us. This was alerting, but also incredibly helpful. I inquired for the name of the school. We're on a clock at this point, so it's time to make moves and get to the bottom of this. After a quick search she told us, "It's, uh, San Francisco University High School. Prep school. That's formal." Immediately I let out a long exhalation of exhaustion. That's like another thirty minute drive. Ugh.

"Welp, we better get on this fast. It's only three, still plenty of time left in the day!" Ellis reminded me, and I unwillingly followed him back into our squad car. The ride there was quite soothing, actually. Got to drive through parts of the city that I haven't seen in a while, and it recalled some past adventures back to my mind. Never before had a case been this intense or meaningful, though. This was something new and entirely estranged compared to my previous endeavors.

"Hey, you think we could turn on something else? Maybe like a jazz station or something. I don't know, blaring rock doesn't really fit the atmosphere right now, you feel?" I shouted to Ellis, and he could barely hear me. I was staring out of the window, motionless, like my mind had escaped the interior barrier of my skull. Like my thoughts had slipped through the walls that confined it to virtuality, breaking all principles of abstraction and its metaphysical characteristics. I had become a spirit, as I pondered the lives of those lost to this murderer. How one person could be so cold, so morally incompetent, so ill. Murder was always beyond me, and I still don't understand it. How lives can just be tossed around and played with, ultimately leading to its disposure. The soul of one person, the person who takes others, and adds these souls to their collection, is really not a soul at all. They feel superior, like their acts are justified by some twisted measure in their head, but in reality, their inferiority is the reason behind the absence of their true heart, their true character. Personality is decency. Sure, charisma can enlighten the joyful nature of one person, and the self-wallowing pity another feels may further add to their rugged and cynical feeling of depression, but that doesn't define us. That's just a mask, worn by us to shell ourselves from revealing our true temperament. At the end of the day, the question of *who are you?* reduces, quite simply, to are you selfish, or are you selfless? Everything else is molded by this essential theory.

I really believe that the truest and most honest revelations come when no effort is being put in to actually having that revelation at all. This recollection of ideas I had experienced while on the trip to the high school really opened my eyes to a new path of empathy. Maybe, it was a dilemma within him, as he takes these lives and commits these crimes, maybe he is in the end questioning his motives, his judgment. Eventually, the dark nature of these atrocities may come back to haunt him. Only time will tell.

We pulled up after about ten more minutes of that god-awful country music to the front of the high school, as the school was still in session it seemed. After school activities, I presume. The deep introspection I underwent during the car ride led to me forgetting to have Ellis actually change the station. I suppose country music is healthy for philosophical practice.

"You awake, Ted?" Ellis said to me, tapping me on the shoulder. I guess I really was out of it. Huh. I shoved his hand away and got out of the car, while he read to me the game plan he thought up, probably during my mental vacation. "Alright, I think we should ask the principal, first, if they have any idea that the victims of these murders were both attendants of this high school. That, probably will lead nowhere, so then I think we ask for the yearbook of their graduating year. Sound good?"

"Junior year, maybe even sophomore. Senior year, probably less clubs. Acceptance to college grants a lack of effort in their final year, possibly leading them to not join a few clubs. If that isn't the case, it may be other factors, but junior year is probably the best choice. Or both would work too," I responded, almost critiqued. I really do hope, however, that we aren't interrupting a school-wide production or anything. And just as I thought this to myself, we turned the corner outside the building and saw a large poster depicting the details of a school-wide play with today's date marked in bold print at the foot of the spectacle. Of course. Something to just block our plans. You've got to do what you've got to do, though.

We stood outside the front entrance, waiting to be buzzed in, and stared at the camera with our badges out. After a few seconds, they let us in, and directed us to a waiting area in the main offices. I surveyed the area. "Looks like a pretty nice school ... hallways seem nice. There has to be more to it. I don't think the killer is a product of their environment, perhaps, maybe their friends betrayed their trust?" I proposed, as Ellis pondered along with me. After a few minutes, the principal came into the room to meet with us.

"Hello, I assume you're here to ask about the recent murders?" she asked us, shaking our hands. We sat back down and proceeded with the conversation.

"Yes, it came across our background research that both victims attended your high school, and we would just like to ask for a copy of some of your yearbooks to aid in our investigation," Ellis began, before I could even begin to get a word out. I like this control he's showing, authority.

"Of course, years?" she responded, willingly, yet remorsefully. Letting her discontempt be known, she gave us a stern look.

"Twenty-o-nine, ten, and eleven, if you could. We could even just take pictures and return them to you today," I ordered, and off she went to the library to retrieve them. After a few minutes she returned with the three books I requested, and said we could take them back to the station. We said our condolences and assured her that we would do everything in our power to stop this killer, and left.

"Damn. You really think high school has something to do with it?" Ellis said to me in the car, as soon as we packed in.

"I don't know man, I really don't. Grudges can be powerful, though, you never know the demons a person may be masking. Blending into the norms of society to protect their own evils from exposure. It's a risky, secretive world," I said, again, philosophically. I truly believe we have something concrete here, at least, in terms of leads. There is no way that the victims sharing a high school is merely a coincidence, it just can't be. Now, we have a long way back from the school to the station. More time to fall asleep, honestly. I began to doze off when I saw my phone light up with a text message from an unknown number. Puzzled, I of course responded with *Who is this?* Only to receive back a message saying *Alice.* That's right.

"Hey, other than this killer, things have been pretty quiet, don't ya think?" Ellis said to me, but I was too tired to multitask, so I simply grunted in response and tried to mumble some words of agreement. I'm now waiting for Alice to text back, curious to see where this road goes. She asked me what I had planned for the night, and so, I had to ask Ellis.

"Hey, whatcha think we're gonna do tonight? I say we just reference the yearbooks to see which of the alumni from this place still live in the area. Probably give us a good lead, eh?" I asked, hoping he would agree with me.

"Yeah, probably sounds good. This killer is leaving like no evidence at the crime — wait! Surveillance cameras from outside Cali 101. Did we check those?" Ellis said in the midst of a revelation.

"I'll get Amber on it right now. Probably a good idea, except we'll only really be able to tell if someone is suspicious or not if they appear to be running out of the building. Otherwise, they'll probably just look normal.

"This is true" Ellis said, and he went on about driving. I looked back down at my phone, and realized I still have to tell Alice my plans. *Probably nothing. Some busy work for a little bit but not much, really. And you?* I still hadn't saved her number into my contacts, should probably do that.

"So, we doing much then?" I asked Ellis, hoping he wouldn't question my motives, "Doesn't seem like we have any evidence or anything to go off of."

"I don't know, you tell me. Seems like it," he responded. Coast appears to be clear. I peered down at my phone to see Alice replied with *Nothing :).* Why not try something new? *Well, how about we do something? Would you want to?* God, my wording was so off. It had been so long since I actually asked a girl out on a date, I'd almost forgotten how. It was like I was doing it for the first time again, except my naïvety may not be mistaken for apprehension or nerve. This may have been a wrong turn, one that leads me to being alone for the foreseeable future. It's been like over a year since I've even been on a date, what do I even do? This question has been stuck in my head all while awaiting her response. Eventually, she texted back, and allowed me to breathe a sigh of relief. Her ambition seems to be as compelling as my curiosity, which leaves room for me to relax. *Sure, dinner? House of Prime Rib, have you ever been there? My FAVORITE place.* it read. This sounds good. I texted back, *I like it. 7:00 sound good?* Should give me a few hours to get some work done.

"Hey, you want to remember I'm here, sir? You've been absorbed by your phone, since when are you like this?" Ellis said to me, which I was barely able to comprehend over its spell that mesmerized me. Technology can be so captivating, it's like it reels you in. Huh.

"Yeah, my apologies. I was just talking to someone." I quickly fired back, he's gonna ask me ab—

"Talking to who? Since when do you do anything other than work and study?"

"Just a friend. I may not have a very respectable social life, but I at least try to have one sometimes, you know. Don't hate on me for trying!" I retorted, laughingly. I've gotta change that reputation.

We got back to the station at around 5:00. It's been a long few days, I need time to relax. I'm hoping tonight is just that, while I pray another murder doesn't occur. Not what I need, I just need a break. Tomorrow, we'll have to get to work on the classmates. Tonight, it's mental stimulation. At some place I've never eaten at either. We finished up a few things at the office, and headed out for the night. Better to get some extra rest today than to cram. I just realized, I never even asked her for her address! I pulled out my phone and right as I was going to text her and ask, I saw a message depicting her address on the screen. This shouldn't mean anything, but for some reason it makes me feel good. I like where this is going.

I pulled my car to the front of her apartment building at 6:54. Slightly early, but I like the worm I suppose. I barely even had to wait for her, which I found all the more assuring. She got into my car, looking very fancy. Thankfully, I happened to dress quite nicely myself, but she still managed to show me up. "You look good, Alice," I said as she got into the car.

"Thank you!" she exclaimed, smiling. Her complex is only a block down from the station, so I could probably even see her after work sometimes. Imagine that.

Our ride to the restaurant was quite a cheerful one. We discussed our lives, day jobs. Millennium Tower, is her place of occupation, lucky. I've always wanted to work in a skyscraper. I mean, I live in one, but not on a high enough floor to suit my desires. She works on the thirty-sixth floor where you can see all of the city and some of Oakland! Now, imagine that! I've always enjoyed the feeling of meeting new people and getting to know them. It feels as if there is so much to learn, so many different paths to explore. Each one could lead to something entirely different from the next, or something eerily similar. It's almost as if you're filling out a part of your mind with information, and the more information you gather, the more intense your emotions become. Part of the reason I try to be charismatic when I can, to continuously fill this space in my mind, this void. After not knowing many people for so long it seems to have left a large hole in my head. One that I perpetually search to fill. I hope, this can change that, even if it seems I may be getting ahead of myself, it's a change of scenery. Never know what could come from that.

We got to the restaurant and I began to follow standard gentleman procedure. This place looks incredibly upscale, luckily I can cover expenses. *Not that I've had anyone else to spend money on,* I thought to myself, daydreaming the shed of a tear. I held her car door open, and later on held the door to the restaurant open for her too. When we got seated, I felt extremely luxurious, this place she's taken me to is really nice. Almost too nice, if I'm being honest. I hope it isn't too expensive... although it has been a while since I spent a little money.

"So how was your day at work?" she initiated conversation with, which I didn't mind. The table we were seated at was right next to a large window, overlooking the street. Pretty calming, really. *The Palomino.* Interesting name.

"Well, it was a day, I guess. Seems to be the story of my life. And you?" I responded, in a trance of acceptance.

"Productive, to say the least. I'm actually surprised at your willingness to spend time with me, you seem to be more along the likes of a rather occupied man, and you're furthering a connection you made in a coffee shop. Earlier today, I might add."

"I've just been lonely for awhile. I figured it would be healthy to change things up a bit, you know? After some time, you forget how stuff like this feels," I said, oddly willing to open up to her. I don't know, she just feels comforting. Maybe I really do need to get out more. I shrugged at my own introspection. She took notice.

"You alright? You seem on edge," she inquired, from a place of seemingly genuine curiosity and innocence.

"Yeah, I'm alright. Why don't you look at what you want to order, don't get caught up in talking to me. This place has a lot of good stuff," I said to her, then realized my mistake. She caught it too.

"You've never even been here!" she exclaimed to me and laughed it off. The waiter eventually came back around with the waters we requested and neither of us had even looked at the menu. Unprepared we were. "So the life of a detective, what did you do today?" she asked me after a few minutes.

"Today was a bit peculiar, more productive than usual. It started with us getting a call of a murder downtown, then we had to examine the scene, and later go ask questions with the highschool of the victim. Pretty long day honestly, how is the life of an accountant?"

"Huh, I wish I could see that much action in a day. I managed the monthly finances for May, not much excitement, really. Being a detective has to be incredibly fascinating, it must be like a new story every day!" she said with unusual enthusiasm. Again, the waiter came around, but this time we were ready. Alice ordered the cheapest thing I could find on the menu, some chicken pasta. *That was nice of her*. I did not do the same, I got ribs.

"You didn't have to order the cheapest thing on the menu, really!" I said to her, feeling somewhat bad for some unknown reason.

"Maybe I wanted pasta!" she yelled back playfully. This was nice, it got my mind off of the case and served as a tranquilizer, if you will. "Are you close to catching the killer? If you don't mind me asking." *Nevermind.*

"We're trying to make connections, but there's minimal evidence left at the scenes. Killer is good, it's gonna be work. At this point, we're just sending out PSA's to keep everyone on their toes and cautious when out and about alone. Why do you ask?" I said, probably intelligently, to ensure my professionalism.

"Just curious and worrisome. I get nervous when I hear about killings, I don't like them!"

"Me either, Alice, me either. After being exposed to crime for some time, seeing some things don't make a dent anymore. But murder will never be one of them. I cannot find it in me to understand it."

"Well, let's not bring down the mood with melancholy police work, let's get to know each other!" she proposed, and I accepted.

"I like the idea. Where have you traveled before?" I asked, something basic to start off. You know, the routine get-to-know-you questions you always start out with.

"You want the truth? Nowhere special. Alabama when I was twelve, Mass for college. Boy, was that quite the venture."

"Oh, really? What college? That's cross country!"

"M.I.T." she responded, *impressive*, I thought to myself. And she's an accountant? What happened? It's probably best I don't ask, especially on the first date.

"Wow, that's incredible. San Diego State for me, wanted to stay in state."

"Ah, I get you. So I never got to ask, actually, how old are you?" she said, with a sort of joyful look, with a hint of nerve I could feel unravelling behind.

"Twenty-four, and yourself?"

"Twenty-four as well! Coincidence, I suppose?" she said, and we shared a laugh. Soon after a bit more conversing about each other's lives, our food came, which looked remarkably delightful. I could tell the bill was to be hefty, though. That's okay. It's the memories and the moments we go on to cherish that matter, right? Money is just paper. *Oh, how I wish that were true.*

"Okay, let me just say, this place was NOT this good last time I came here." she said, gleefully, and the dinner carried on pretty smoothly. We wrapped up dinner and the bill came out to be $74.32, which I guess is fine. Hopefully, *it* ends up being worth it. We exited the building and proceeded back toward my car, sharing another upbeat conversation on the way there. We got into my vehicle, already started, not even realizing how late we had actually stayed at the restaurant!

"Wow, it's nine thirty, we should probably get going! I can't believe we stayed there for that long just talking, it didn't even seem like time was flying by that fast," she said, noticing that it was way later than either of us had expected it to be. I floored the gas pedal and zoomed out of the parking lot. Luckily, the suspension kept the car relatively smooth and motionless. We had to get home quick, it was like a twenty-five minute drive!

"Hey, it's getting late, do you want to crash at my house? I live right by the station, I'm sure it wouldn't be too big of a deal, plus you wouldn't have to drive so much. Just want to make things easier."

"Luckily, I carry a spare uniform in my car. I would like to accept your offer, if you would be so kind. Thank you," I said to her, truly grateful. A good night's rest? It had been too long since I felt one of those. At least, that's what I thought I was going to feel ...

• • •

I walked into the station the next morning quite unprepared. Oddly acquiescent for my usual behavior, and slightly dizzy from the prior night's ambition. Even with a fresh uniform on that I hadn't worn in six months at least, it still felt untidy. Probably the absence of the morning coffee. *I really need to lay off.* But, at least I was able to sleep in twenty minutes later than usual. As soon as I got into the office, I was bombarded with reports from Amber.

"Okay, I did some scanning on the database over the names of everyone from the yearbooks, turns out that there's still fifty-seven of the people from those three years who live in San Francisco, and twelve others who moved to Oakland. Sorting by the grade level of both the victims, I made a list with the seventeen at the top. I'd roll with this, seems to be the most solid lead we have."

"Do you think it's enough to send police protection?" Ellis asked, more specifically, asked me.

"Not yet, I don't think it's reasonable yet. This is really the only evidence we have to go on, it could end up being just a coincidence." I figured this is probably going to end up being a stretch anyways, it is most likely not too wild of a chance that both victims have lived in San Fran for some time, considering they were both killed here. "We should probably give it an hour or two, though, no?" I asked Ellis, Amber, and a few other people in the room for assurance, considering it's 8:00 in the morning. I don't think many people are up yet.

"Hey, we got another case, anyway. Robbery in East Cut, Fremont and Mission," Amber informed us, *of course.*

"Why do things like this have to happen? Like, why can't we just solve this case without other disturbances?" I said, really annoyed. "Any casualties?"

"Nope, just a casual breaking and entering. Security tape footage though." She showed us the tape, depicting clearly two men with masks sprinting off from the scene. As they dashed away, I thought I noticed something peculiar.

"How'd you get this anyway, and can you zoom in and slow it down, it looks like he drops something." I said, pointing to the screen. A card seemed to have slipped from his pocket as he took off. *Bet it's an I.D.*

"Well, I was on the night shift when it got called in, and so I decided to give the bank a call and ask for their security tape. I figured they'd be willing to help without issuing a warrant, since it was their bank that was robbed, you know?" she said as she zoomed in on the man. Definitely a card of some sort that he dropped. We should probably get over there. I motioned for Ellis to follow me as I jogged out of the station and hopped in the squad car. *Fremont and Mission. We can speed a little bit right?*

"Hey, you might want to slow down a little bit. I mean, it's an important case and all but it's not worth speeding over is it? At least, not twenty over," Ellis reminded me, as I continuously augmented the velocity. I took my foot off the gas for a second, it was only a thirty-five zone, fifty-five probably appears to be quite inappropriate. We arrived at the bank shortly after this awkward conversation, and sure enough, the card was still there.

"That's lucky, it is an I.D." *Jackson Maxwell.* This turned out to be much easier than I had anticipated, allotting me a longer duration to focus on the case of greater consequence. And that's when it hit me.

"Ten thirty four. Amber, we got an I.D. at the scene, Jackson Maxwell," Ellis radioed back to the station as I showed him the card. Unfortunately, I won't be able to join him in bringing the man into questioning, assuming we can find him. She informed us of the address that Mr. Maxwell currently resides at.

"Ten thirty six, I won't be able to bring him in, I have a family thing. That okay?" I asked into the radio, hoping for not too violent of backlash. Amber gets sort of angered by things like this, but she'll understand, I'm confident.

"You didn't bother to tell me?" Ellis said, with a similar tone.

"I'm sorry, I forgot! They say the memory is the second thing to go." I said, humorously to lighten my forgetfulness. He didn't fall for it, and we rode back to the station in relative silence, except for one question that arose.

"Wait, it's eight thirty in the morning. What family thing do you have? If you don't mind me invading your personal space."

"I just have to check on my mom, nothing too bad."

"She okay?"

"Yeah, just she's a little sick right now and sleeping a lot during the day. I figure this is probably the best chance I have to hold a conversation with her, they have her on strong medicine. I'll be back by the time we start going through that list," I responded, slightly hesitant to say.

"I'm so sorry, I wish her a speedy recovery. I'll bring the man in and question him, if you catch the tail end of the interrogation, that would be convenient," he said, sincerely but at the same time, professionally.

Upon our return to the parking lot, I parted from him and started for my car. Luckily, my mother was only a few blocks away, so I should be able to make it back within the hour. *He'll be able to handle it, right? I believe in him.* It's rare that Ellis has to do a certain job without my assistance, but this may prove to be a turning point in his confidence. He accepted the challenge this time around and embraced its difficulty with welcome.

When I arrived at my mother's house, it brought to me a sense of nostalgia. Even though I hadn't grown up here, it's always been heartwarming to revisit this place, rekindling memories that eventually fade with time. I think, truly, that it's the trigger of emotion, knowing my parents live here, that enforces my recollection of my childhood. Just the simple remembrance of them breeds a smile across my face, even in the most grim or somber times. My father greeted me the same way he always does.

"How's it going, son?" Same words, different day. Nice to say, though, that I'm doing good. Grateful.

"I'm pretty good, how about yourself?" I threw back at him, entering the home. I still know my way around it, and I followed him up to the room where she rested as he explained to me his latest projects with bemusing yet passionate enthusiasm. I walked into the room behind him and gave my mother a gentle hug and kiss on the head, as my way of greeting with heartfelt compassion.

"How have you been, Teddy?" she asked me. It felt nice to hear her call me that, and it felt okay to respond again. *Should I mention Alice to them? Or might that complicate things...* I pondered. Back and forth in my mind the question was tossed, while I caught the feeling that I may be getting ahead of myself. I resigned to keeping the conversation less about me and more about them for the rather short duration of my stay.

We spoke for a short deal of time that felt like ages, and I planned my departure to be dear, but the urgency of Ellis's message encouraged my swiftness. Even still, the joyous nature of my visit helped to lift my spirits, something I've felt was necessary after all of the gloom that throws itself over my dayjob. *Another entry into the files of the lost, damn it* I thought to myself as I said my goodbyes, and raced back to the station to pick him up. *How many murders?*

We got to the scene of the crime with little information to go on, but it was the same as we'd seen as of late. Classical murders, presumably the same group of people that attended the high school some time ago. It's unfortunate, really, that this serial monster must take these lives like this, but it's even more frustrating and disappointing that we can't do anything about it. I let the team know my rage, "We've got to do something. Now!" I yelled, in fury.

"We are trying, there seems to be nothing here. Just a clean slit to the throat and the body thrown into the abyss of the alley. Probably happened over night, killer probably slipped into the victim's apartment, did the business, and dropped him right here. Took off down the lane and vanished into the madness of the city. Unreal that it happened so close to the station, only a few blocks away,." Ellis analyzed, trying to reason with my anger, but he only managed to foment the flame of my exasperation.

Alice I recalled, in a panicked rush of fear. *What if the killer had gotten to her too?* I fumbled with my phone as I dialed the digits of her contact, with the anxiety settling in. I am not supposed to let my work interfere with my personal life, but if it's someone's life at risk, I guess I can allow them to coincide respectfully. My duty, after all, is to protect the community.

Ring. Ring. Ring. No answer.

The panic crept into my attention with intrusive force. The adrenaline was beginning to set in and it was overtaking my reasonable limitations. I contemplated booking it for my car to drive to her work place, until an innocent text message saved me from irrationality. A simple *Can't call right now, in a meeting.* Reassuring, but unfair.

"Hey, you want to help with the investigation, maybe?" Ellis shouted, as I had begun to stray from the scene. I steadily returned to the group, forgetting at the time to respond to Alice. After a few minor inspections of the scene, we decided to I.D. the casualty. As morbid as it may seem, another death from the same high school may work to our favor, more evidence against the killer, possibly. At this point, honestly, I don't know what to do with this case anymore. It has spiralled into a doubtful string of fatalities, and I'm just hoping the killer just makes a crucial mistake we can exploit.

Another hour of aimless searching led to no additions to our current pool of knowledge on the case. Eventually, we chalked it up to the rest of them, and later an identification confirmed our suspicions that it correlated with the previous convictions of this mysterious high school killer. After a while longer we began investigating the names on the list, and as I peered over the totality of it, I noticed something oddly peculiar upon my surveillance. Alice's name was on the list! I figured it would be best not to bother her at work with a call, so I prompted to text her first. *So, you went to San Francisco University High School?*

We resolved to beginning our interrogations, and agreed on running through the list alphabetically. Only seventeen names, it is likely that we can finish a good deal of them within the time constraints of the day. I squinted to my left wrist to check my watch, *2:00.* Luckily, I am not expecting much tonight with Alice, allowing me to focus more on the case. It'd been a while since we got to some good police work.

"Let's get to it," Ellis called to me, and we mobilized. As we departed from the area, second thoughts on my fidelity to the mission began to arise, and I wrestled with these ideas for some time. I'm still at a loss in regards to the integrity of privately interviewing Alice, but I feel it may be an obligation. As long as I have the list, Ellis wouldn't have to know *every* name on it, right? *Maybe I should just do the interview with him at my side, just a warning to her should suffice.*

• • •

The third house produced similar leads to the preliminary two. A few names of significant bullies from their times in high school. I assume it's simple feelings of disillusion they experience when we remind them of these questions, and I believe I could extrapolate the rest of the list. They aren't thinking of the right people, though. It's not the bully that would go on and do these operations, it's the bullied. Vengeance, when the most dangerous person wields it, can be the most unpredictable weapon. When the mind is equipped with such a vicious apparatus, only the omniscient can forsee the expectant events. Not even they who wield its might know the following path they will take. These people we have interviewed don't see it. They look back on their periods of high school and remember the villainous nature of these specimens, but obstruct their memory from these minor details. *Maybe one will see it.*

We continued on down the list, and got a few more names to research once we returned back to the station. Soon. Alice's name is coming up on the list. We've only three left before hers, and I do think she will be off of work by then. She has thanked me for warning her of our inevitable arrival. I welcomed her grace, but was careful not to seem accusative. This should not impede our relations.

The list is actually piling up quite remarkably, relatively in-depth characteristic and behavioral descriptions accompany a fair amount of the names on the list, which will prove incredibly resourceful when we begin our true research. I am maintaining the thought that this case will ease up sooner or later, but worry is beginning to build up at an equal pace. How could such brutal and intensive crimes mask the puppeteer of these lives in such an elusive disguise? Because the scariest veracity of them all, happens to be that this killer is out there hidden in plain sight. Hiding in the city, a population of thousands, amongst the common man, invisible to the detective eye. This truth irks me.

Again, puzzled beyond relief, I am finding it difficult to see the ending of this thing. It has only been a few days, but three deaths in that short span of time, *absurdity*. Who could it be?

"God, man, you got any ideas? I'll be damned if we don't find something soon!" Ellis explained to me, curiously I envied his composure. At first, the exclamation came off with a twist of aggression, but it relaxed into sincerity shortly after hearing it. The atmosphere he conveyed was really indescribable, it was almost reassuring. While it shouted to me to keep my composure, it also seemed to grasp for assistance. Like he is eyeing defeat and perseverance at the same time, struggling with which diverged path to take.

"I'm not sure. It has to be something that's been planned for quite some time, though. Probably of someone with a higher level of intelligence. Three murders like these don't just happen without any planning."

It was almost a rhetorical response. *Of course it took planning*. But there was something about this string of deaths, that just screamed to me. As I examined each body and scene, I could hear the screeches of assessment, of this satanic character willfully theororizing these executions. It bothers me, the inhumanity.

Finally, we came across Alice's name on the list, and we arrived at her home which was no more than walking distance from the police station. With open policy, we gestured to come inside as she greeted us at the door and made it a rather colloquial meeting. I could see the genuine fear in her eyes, anxiety of uncertainty. *You and I both, Alice* I fancied, and she received, unimaginably.

I hadn't known that she attended the same school as the other victims, and I was curious to see if she had made the connection as well. It's a bit of a dark thing, knowing that lost lives likely have a common overlap in their histories, all at the same place of her studies just a few years back. It's astounding to see the change of such characters over such a relatively short span of time. Interestingly, I've given it some thought, and came to realize recently that maybe it isn't necessarily a change in personality, rather something acting upon it to reveal it. There is more to this theory, I have discovered, and I'll indulge in the hypothesis more deeply.

The ways that humans behave, the struggles they experience, and the methods they utilize to overcome them, I have found, can truly be related to other natural perfections of the realm of science. For instance, a human being may have a mental state that acts in correspondence to Newton's First Law, such that states that "every object will remain at rest or in uniform motion in a straight line unless compelled to change its state by the action of an external force". In essence, this can be deduced to the requirement of a spark to cause change in a person's state of mind. A spark, as in, something to awaken an inner revelation, or epiphany, that can disturb the tranquility of their disposition.

Associatively, these fragments of mental equilibria can appear as brittle as the steel of the most fragile sword or convey the strength of the shoulders in which Atlas held the world upon. In either instance, the cause of disturbance can vary among infinite possibilities, and conversely could have such an impact as to drastically alter one's psychology and permanently taint their cognitive abilities or faintly brush the interior obstruction to their stubborn character.

Where am I going with this? Well, ironically enough, my abstract philosophy may have actually led me to discern more about my occupation, specifically the case we are working now: homicide. See, what I've come across is that sometimes this intellect can't be suppressed. It is not impossible that the friendly picket fence neighbor may also be the serial killer evading capture. But then again, the same person on death row might be sworn to innocence but thrown under an incriminated rap. Our demons may be our true characters after all, when exposed to the right opportunities. Subsequently, our angels may not always be able to overcome our demons; our virtue we behold with such radiance may ultimately succumb to the vacuuming pressure of our vice. Blinded by the wicked beam of darkness our innate savagery may shine on us could be our compassion struggling to prevail, merely guided from evasion of failure.

Finding the key to the balance between our demons and our angels, our id and our superego, may be what unlocks the doors to common health in daily interactions. Until we learn to arrest the serenity of our focus and drown out our distractions, this dream may be unperceivable. The bliss of a mannered society that the populous seems to desperately chase and retort simultaneously could be approached from a much more simplified angle, but the average person will continue to fantasize about this Nirvana of world peace, with false hopes that it could ever actually be true. Anyways, I have explained the theory for too long.

Our confrontation went as expected, Alice was essentially useless as the other names on the list before her. Just random names that have no relation to one another disregarding the university high school. That's what all of these have been. Useless pointers in the wrong directions. *We need a breakthrough, seriously.*

I stormed out of the room with an ambitious stomp to my step, and I imagine Alice could feel the vexation I emitted through the vibrations I caused in the floor. I envisioned the linoleum of her kitchen floor rattling from my frustration, possibly sending her into a panicked sensation of distress. I can feel the frigid heart of this serial killer creeping into my thoughts. Their darkness seeping in, contaminating my cerebral processes. I have tried looking at this case analytically and empathetically, but none of it is giving me any leads. Nothing I inspect brings me any closer to any sort of a development. *It's rising.*

This volcanic ferocity I've recently found, I'm trying to convert it into crisp attention to finding this man. This struggle I continue to find with myself, there's just too many layers to it. It's been a couple of days, but there have been lives lost. It's like we're at war with this monster. The police force versus the killer, and currently the perpetrator is tactfully escaping our efforts.

I cannot comprehend the state of being of those close to the ones whom we have lost, but I can definitely say that I feel the loss. The agony that formulates from the deceased, it isn't just the lifelessness that gets to me. It's the lost opportunity and unwilling extraction of *what could have been.*

I've got to learn to tune this population of agitated thoughts out. I ought to return to my work, with a clearer mind and more streamlined focus. I owe it to the dead. We pulled back into the station and I prepared the team for our forthcoming endeavours: a determined succession of labor in which no one will give up. *We will find the link, the evidence, the missing piece that ties us to the killer.* I ordered everyone to meet in the hall of the station, and I began my speech.

"We just got a list of possible persons of interest from some interviews around town, I know it has been a long day, believe me, it has been for me too. But that does not mean we are going to let this killer win. We have our job to do, and that job is to protect this city. They think we have no way of finding out who they are, but believe me, no crime is perfect. There is a link, and we will find it. That is a promise."

In all honesty, though short, it was probably one of the most certifying addresses I've given, especially with where we are in this case. I believe in our team though, and I believe in my efforts to piece this evidence together. Tonight, I must comprise a list of possibilities and rank it in descending order of suspicion. Names that come up on the list multiple times, of course, should be of higher priority. This, along with analysis of each of the previous murders has to turn up something. I warned each of the people we interviewed to keep an eye out for anyone that may be an immediate danger to them and to notify us if they feel threatened. I silently plead with you, murderer,, *if you have a heart, stop this now. It's too much.*

• • •

A long night of work, leaving the station at nearly midnight, I'm due for a rest. It's been such a great deal of time since I've had the opportunity to message Alice, I dearly hope she's been alright. This case is of such relevance to her, I haven't had the chance to speak a word since we were in her quarters, but I assume she is fine.

I texted her a simple, *Hey, when you get this in the morning, we should have a date again tomorrow. We could both use a bit of fun in our lives*, but the panic began to set in as I pressed send. This seems to be a good, though rapid, thing I have going for me here. I do not intend to screw it up, like my other obligations may. I have a poor history of that, one I would prefer not to recall.

I stopped at the liquor store, the one that never fails to be open, on the way home. Luckily, I've just enough on me to get a bottle. It has been some time since I had a drink, but I would not argue that I've earned it. *You've got to treat yourself here and there*, I thought to myself, in reality as an excuse. When I arrived at my living room with the bottle, I poured one glass to drink, but only made it about halfway through before passing out. The rest shall be enjoyed tomorrow, possibly after our date. For now, my imagination shall steer for me.

The fantasy began amongst a prairie of great length with beautiful flora scattered about. I illustrated a forest along its edges, surrounding the gracious flatland, one I felt stretched endlessly into the horizon. I looked about for company, eager to explore, and found but a girl. A woman, I feel as though I have met before. Her countenance appears to be unfamiliar, but something in the aura around her invokes a feeling of trust, of connection. I walked to her.

As I approached her, my pace underwent diminuendo. I took her hand as if I had claimed it my own, and we began to wander. It's truly surreal. It's art. It's untrue yet so alive. Wondrous of her beauty, I slowed our steps. Savoring her presence, I examined the outskirt of the woodland, searching for a pathway we could take. Soon enough, my eyes stumbled upon it, and I guided our dance in its general direction. Even with intent, our movement felt motionless. Her mystery soon evanescent, and her spiritual integrity so defined.

Leading her on the trail, we both remained silent. It was as if our communication was unobstructed with words unnecessary, but we understood each other's desires. Her character did not flaw me into tyranny, she was rather submissive in her nature, a truth that astounded me. How a being of such obtainable perfection could be so timid. Furthermore, how I could recognize such limitless excellence, was beyond the restrictions of my intelligence. We carried on, as the sky shifted to the black swallows of night and returned to its transparent blue of the day, parading through the course with an audience astray.

Her omnipotent gaze, I observed, appeared fluorescent among the dull pattern of forestry arrangements, as we halted our desultory wander. As I recorded her virtual luxury, I speculated upon her true origins. Impressed in my mind are the unique perplexities her glare offered, those I fear I will inevitably long for.

At the conclusion of this path came a small house upon a mound, with nothing more than a beaten down garden outside of it. The repeated till of cultivation has worn down the soil, deteriorating its natural ability. The stones directing other travellers to the home's entrance have been misplaced and eroded, and the grass of the yard overgrown. We mutually agreed to walk toward the entrance, curious of its tenancy. Before we could knock on the door, however, it opened. An elderly man, noticeably wise, emerged from the dim interior. He confronted us with an uptight warmth, and he seemed quite excited that we had shown up at his door.

"Where from are y'all?" he asked us with an explicitly distinct dialect. Neither of us explained where he had came from, because neither of us actually knew. He invited us in, and began to inform us of a tale. A regional tale, I presume, of classical folklore.

"It was three of us, you see. Caught up in a hiking trip we were lost about. Confused in the middle of nowhere, we searched for safety. It was a stormy night, lots of rain. Lots of thunder. Lots of lightning in the woods. We didn't want to be trapped in the rain so we took shelter underneath a cave in this very hill," he started, which at first caught my attention, but I soon allowed my attention to doze off. He carried on with his anecdote regardless, as I was occupied with her majesty.

"I pointed out that there was really not much in this cave, and that our resources were in the tent away. 'We ought to go back for our stuff,' I said, expecting them to follow us. I waited a bit for them to follow me, and it took a bit of pulling them over to come with, but we ventured off into the storm. The winds picked up as we took off, and I realized soon that it was probably ill-advised. Still, I carried on, not knowing what I had gotten myself into. We needed this for hospitality, you see? The rest of my guys, I swear, were right behind me," he continued, and as his little story went on I could feel a chilling boom in my spine. One I nervously tried to ignore as the sweat began to collect in the upper portion of my shirt. My grip on the girl's hand tightened.

"I said, 'This is probably not the best idea, but we're too far into it now to turn around.' And right as I noticed one of them had gone missing, I saw that we were in trouble. We picked up the pace and hurried to the supplies before agreeing on turning back for him, you see, that's when the other mate with us vanished along with him. I was panicking at this point, you see—" he began to rush, and now I'm feeling the anxiety. Disillusioned from the beauty I had been introduced to, I struggled to see the reality of this fantasy, and how its intricacies had come to life. Just then, as he approached this segment of his narrative, I felt it. Her hand disappeared from my grasp, and mine slipped through where hers used to be. *I've lost her.* Quickly, the feelings set in, one after another. Set in stone. He was finishing his story but it was too much at once for me to comprehend what he was saying in the moment. Panic. Fear. Guilt. Worry. Confusion.

I stared at him with awe as he returned a gaze of emptiness. It was a look I had not yet been familiar with, and one that took me some time to understand its intentions. The reality of it was not there, rather, it seemed vastly unreal. A look that felt as if it had so much to say, but no power to say it. A look that puzzled me in this unconscious moment. A look that I would not soon forget, and cherish its complexity once I awoke. And then, in an instant, it all vanished.

— Three Weeks Pass —

As I walked into the kitchen, I noticed that Alice had taken upon herself the duty of making breakfast. I hadn't asked her to do so, but she insisted. Over the past few weeks, our connection has grown ever so strongly. I have noticed that she's been more open to discussing her past, and I as well. There are many nights in a week now where we will stay up drinking and playing rummy with the casual sitcom playing on the TV in the background as we push aside our leftover dinner from the day before. I prefer her place, typically, as my home is not the largest. I hadn't given situations like these thought when I was buying it.

"It's ready, Teddy. Your favorite," she said to me, with a tempting smile. She turned around with a setting of pancakes drowned in a lite syrup, proving her accuracy. As she arranged the meal on the table in the room adjacent to the kitchen, I poured two glasses of orange juice for us both. *Orange juice is her favorite.* Walking over to the table to eat, she took notice.

We discussed our days ahead of us with solid enthusiasm, but both of us particularly focused on the breakfast. Luckily, I had prepared for a rather light day of relaxing. It's been a few weeks since the last murder and the case seems to have taken a break, at least for now. We are still working to make connections on it every so often, but the trail is very limited. Thus, I don't need to do any at-home work. Hopefully, the killer at least turns up, just in a less violent way. We need something to go off of, not just intuition.

"What do you have going on tonight?" I asked, in hopes her response would be *nothing*. Unfortunately, this was not the case.

"Family party over in Oakland, I think I'm gonna be busy the whole night. I'm sorry." she said, vividly apologetic.

"Oh, don't apologize, love. It's nothing to worry about, have fun with family. On that note, I might go and visit mine actually. You need a ride over there?" I asked, partially out of generosity, and partially out of my own interests.

"I should be okay, thanks though. Can I just take the day off?" she inquired, lightheartedly changing the subject. I pondered its possibility, then shuffled to her room to get my change of clothes. She followed, and I didn't mind.

"You know, don't be alarmed if you get a call at some point during the day, or tomorrow, or the work days after that," she told me, "I might get bored, you know?"

"Why not? The station has been a ghost town lately, I'm not entirely sure why. It's like the one case we had a while ago, the killer just got distracted or something. Other than that, it's been quiet. I don't mind it, less work for me."

We sauntered out of her home ignorant of the time. We made it no worry to us if she was to be late. We still were going to assume appropriate responsibility, but taking our time entrusted my deep affection in hopeful ethos. She followed me aimlessly to my car, with a loose grip on my hand. I didn't make an effort to let go, and for a moment we just stood outside my car, hands interlocked, gazing into each other's eyes. At the end of this moment, we agreed on a smile and the entry into the vehicle.

"You know, I think the best thing about living here, really, is the nice weather," she began, as a form of small talk. I didn't mind, because she was most definitely right, but the idea of weather actually sparked a train of thought for me, one whose tracks led down the road of paradise. Now, it may be early and all, but I could really use a vacation to get away from police work for some time. Just an idea, for now, nothing more.

I dropped her off at her work and she thanked me for the ride, and as I kissed her goodbye, I came to the realization that I was going to miss her for the majority of the day. Probably, when I'm drenched in papers, I'm going to be thinking of her and staring at the wall with her flooding my mental portraits. Not the worst compromise of love but certainly the most distracting.

Of course, the remedy of this love leaves me in a healthier state, but it is not one I can take for granted. I do feel blessed, however, to have found such a brilliant woman who likes me as I like her. I thought it would be a great luxury and some time before I found myself in this situation, but it seems to have stumbled upon me with welcoming temptation. As of late, I cannot recall a tragedy I've experienced. It has been weeks since another murder in the cursed case, I feel as if the killer has either retired from his deeds or relocated. Either way, I am grateful no more lives have met their end. *Knock on wood.*

It's a Saturday, a day to recuperate. I've needed a break from the rather spontaneous lifestyle I've grown accustomed to, where I'm taking part in a fair amount of activity. Today, however, I've decided on doing something for myself. *Surprising.* There is a well-received cross country race taking place in the area—a high school competition. Many runners of the state placed their bids to join, and I'd be interested to spectate. Of the many things I don't do in my spare time, sporting events miss the list. I am always prepared to indulge in an event for quality entertainment.

The race starts at 10am, so I ought to head towards it now to get better parking. I started toward the field, and realized as I approached I'd be walking some distance before I got to the actual course. Many people had a similar idea.

It's hot—only eighty degrees or so—but a radiant humidity blanketed the meadow. These kids are going to be very shocked when they start racing, I recall—I dearly hope they're hydrated. It leads me to reminisce, these races, I should attend them more often. High school was the glory days, really, sometimes I wish I could go back. Although much of my time was spent partying heavily at Jack Thompson's house down the street and sprinting out the winding trail through the forest of his backyard on Saturday nights or staying up until 2:30 in the morning finishing research papers I had failed to commit to when assigned them earlier in the month, it was still an era of my life I choose not to forget. Perhaps, it is because of the constant feeling of unease that flooded my thoughts day in and day out, never knowing whether or not I would get called down to the Dean's office for my leisure activities, or if I was going to lose my shot at eclipsing prestige once I began my college days. More realistically, however, I believe it was the truth of wasted potential. While I made sure to keep mostly A's in my classes, I still could have achieved more. It haunts me, to this day, knowing that I finished seventh in my class and I could have easily finished first. It haunts me.

—

Academics weren't the only promise I held, it was in athletics where I held promise as well. This talent dated back to even further than high school: middle school is where it began. The yearly gym class mile, where I was able to discover my aerobic gift. I never really ran much outside of the occasional parking lot basketball with a couple of my friends, but I managed to stay in moderate shape. 5:23 was the time I aimlessly jogged, and unexpectant of my talents at the time, I shrugged off the school record as a side activity. *Oh, I wish I hadn't.*

My lack of discovery carried on to high school, especially with freshman year. While my intelligence had been something I was aware of, it had not really been something I capitalized on. I got by with weak studies and half-attempted assignments, enough so that my parents didn't yell at me. My running career was the same, lack of motivation. I would try some of the practices and just run the race as I would. I forget the times but they were average, I had thought. *More of the same.*

It was my senior year where I realized how much I had messed up. I never really paid attention to running until the summer before my last year, when my coaches finally convinced me to do it in the offseason. I decided why not try giving it *some* effort, but quickly I became fascinated with the idea of maximum. So as the season progressed, I began to find a passion for the sport, and I felt my anticipation for the season rise. Cross country awaited.

The season was not what I had expected it to be, especially with how much I grew to love it. My times dropped every race, and the state race was the most fun of them all. Track season, I hoped, would be even better. Training through the winter wasn't bad, and the spring had even more greatness in store. The high school I attended was famous for its school's running history, and I began to want to join the line of history established already. My name, I wanted, was to have a résumé of excellence. I couldn't wait.

The season opened on fire: 4:19 to start the season in the mile. It was history in the making, I saw. I'm not sure where the gene for running was in me, to my knowledge my parents weren't outstanding. General luck, I guess. By the state meet in track, I was at 4:01 and ready to break 4. I'd be with rare company of those who had broken 4 in the mile, and I had all the mental preparation necessary. *It's time.* I continued to tell myself it was time to implant my name in history, and these thoughts raced faster as I lined up at the start.

"Ready... set..." *Bang.*

The gunshot sounded at the finals of the mile, and I knew what I had to do. I went through the first lap in 0:57, good pace, a little fast, but not terribly. Second lap I came back and the time was 1:58.61, *gotta pick it up.* I'd been in this situation before, and always forgot to expel the right amount of energy here. I threw in a surge, already ahead of the pack, to get on pace for 3:59. I didn't realize my mistake until I saw the clock at 2:54 when I came back around. *56 might be too fast. Gotta push.* I thought to myself the worst, but just tried to power through. I could feel the lactic acid building up in my legs, and the wall was starting to come closer. I peered at the clock at the 1400m mark, it read 3:30. I had to go.

I don't think I'll ever be able to forgive myself for it. I see now that if I trained as hard as I did that year for every year, I could've smoked 3:55. But instead, I was stuck with a 4:02 off a dead 68 on my final lap. I didn't realize that I was so close until I crossed the finish line a state champion. *Failure.* I had a chance to make history and my incompetent work ethic held me back. A day that shines bright in my memory as *What could've been.* I had hoped tasting glory at this level would intrigue me to strive for greater things as I carried on, but it failed to do so. I'm still that same unmotivated, selfish-at-heart, lazy eighteen-year old. It forever haunts me: I never broke it.

—

Anyways, running will reside in my heart still, I find it hard to imagine it ever leaving. I enjoyed it too much that year to forget it. I, in a way, envied the runners of today, seeing them compete at such a high stage with great competition. I miss it, truthfully. *Enough of the reflection.*

The gun fired and before the dauntless, captivated eyes of the runners I watched was a course with boundless hills and grassy terrain, much of which providing obstacle and struggle on the quest for PRs. I heard the announcer say from the four-wheeler pacemaker that the top time attendee ran a 14:27. *Oh, Cali.*

I chased the front of the pack around the course wherever I had the chance to watch, just like the old days, with the stopwatch timing them. They went through the first mile marker in 4:50, slow for PRs but probably accurate for the course. As soon as they went through the first mile, a runner in blue from the back of the pack of seven shot up to the front and didn't stop. They kept a moderate lead of about 25 meters heading into the second mile and the reminiscence began again. I watched as he negative split with a 4:47, and I cheered on his perseverance, hoping he would keep pace.

The final 350m straightaway approached the runners and it was that same kid taking home the gold at 14:49, as he was seeded 1st. Quite impressive, honestly. This day made me miss running quite a lot. Almost to the point where I contemplated going for a jaunt of my own, but I decided against it. I had some reading to catch up on, particularly on a new detectivity book that was just published. I stuck around at the course for awhile, running into a few coaches I had known during my career, before packing up. I headed home the normal route and picked up a bottle of rum on the way back to indulge in tonight. *Drink for celebration, not for depression.*

With a recent uptake in alcohol, I expected it to have an effect on my health, but I feel relatively fine. I guess it's the high of life suppressing the toxins, or I'm really just built for heavier consumption, I don't know. Either way, I'm enjoying it. I hadn't really been able to experience partnered drinking much until I met Alice, and she showed me the pleasure it can give. *How lucky I am.* Only part that sucks is its expense, *of course*. Why do all things we enjoy have to cost so much money? I swear it runs the world.

As I drove home from the liquor store, I couldn't throw the thoughts of running and what it was to me out of my head. My wasted potential stuck, engraved in my mind, as I coursed the street toward home. First night in a while where I'm not with her, and I've almost forgotten what to do with myself. I guess I'll read, but at this moment I feel vacant without her. She's probably off doing her usual activities, and I'm here pondering how to use up my time.

When I stepped inside my apartment, I threw my pocket's contents on the table and started for my room before the ringing of my phone echoed through the hallway and landed in my ear. I jogged back to the table to pick it up and saw that it was Ellis. Curiously, I picked it up, and he informed me of another murder. The finding of a body always puzzled me, in a sense; what would my reaction be? I always wondered how I would take it, not knowing it would be there. Death always disturbed me! I slammed the phone on the table and stormed out of the room, forgetting my wallet, which only led to more pent up anger. I was sure I had broken the door to my room after the second shutting, and as I rode the occupied elevator down to the first floor, I assumed the passengers could see the steam puffing from my ears. In my head was the shouting of voices, furious at this killer. *I thought we figured this out? No more murders. Here we are, another one.* Much of the internal noise was intelligible anyway and didn't make sense. It was the flushing of these thoughts that cleared my head as I arrived at the station and jumped in the squad car with Ellis. Thankfully, the ride there alone was enough to keep the voices down for at least a few hours, until I could let it out with Alice on a call. *Or should I?.*

That was always a dilemma in my mind, whether or not I should seek to vent my frustration with her or someone else or if I should keep it in. On one hand, I feel as if it is necessary for self-maintenance that I express these thoughts in some way, so that they stray toward rationality. On the other hand, however, it seems needy and unwanted of me, crying to other people about my problems. I never kno—nevermind.

We got to the scene and it was similar to the others. It's 4:00 now, probably 2:00 when it took place. Hour to get the body to the alley, another hour for it to be discovered. The work seems oddly like the ones of the killer from a few weeks ago—*precise* and clean. I marvelled at the death's origins, it seems to have been by drugging. The name tag on the man said William, employee at GAP, presumably a few blocks away. My initial thought was to scan the list of names we used for a William, but when I alerted Sophie, Amber's replacement for the day since she's sick, she got back to us saying the name didn't match. This couldn't be right; I barked at her to check again. She came back with the same result and I panicked. Anyways, I whipped out my phone and dialed Alice as fast as I could. *No answer, family party.* I figured, so I resorted to a text message asking her to assure me she's okay. Murders always send my mind into a frenzy, I swear it.

Now the name might not have been on the list, so I ordered Sophie to check if he went to the same high school as the others, San Francisco University. There was still no match, meaning this killer is a different pattern than the others. Possibly another killer, or possibly the one we already suspected switching up motives. We have work to do now.

A few minutes of impatient thinking passed before an anonymous tip came in, and instantly Sophie notified me. It said that the person heard struggling in an abandoned building adjacent to the scene of the crime, and that they were just trying to help where they can. Cautious, Ellis and I headed over to investigate.

When we parked the car outside of the tower, it was obvious that it was deserted. The dull, cookie-cutter facade portrayed a ghostly look to the structure, and the absence of lights provided enough evidence that an ominous vibe was present. Cold to the touch, the walls seemed to want to crumble upon the slightest reverberation, although the foundation said otherwise. I wondered for a moment the activities that have gone on here: the criminal meetings and escapes, the potential killing of William Jamison, all of it. Its history that I was unfamiliar with astounded me, especially how its fundamental image is copied in various buildings in other locations. Doesn't every city have *that* building? At least, I've seen it in all of the cities I have visited. Anyways, back to the task at hand.

Classic search and check, we approached the entry. We went in, and I shined my flashlight around, seeing nothing. It seems to have been an industrial building at one point, but now its emptiness proves otherwise. Discarded remnants of drug deals (plastic bags and soda cans) crowd the space of the floor. No one regularly inspects the place for sanitary conditions, so critters have infested themselves where they can. We proceeded toward the staircase, and started our way up.

"Doesn't seem like there's anything here? Is it?" Ellis called to me as we paced quickly. I agreed.

"Probably gonna be some homeless people living on the floors above. Don't be frightened, they won't hurt you," I said back, wondering if that was what the person who called in the tip was reporting, just another way of doing so. It's shelter, they need it, I don't mind.

A few floors up we found an empty syringe and an unloaded gun, but nothing else that was really of value. We concluded that something probably had gone down here at some point, but in regards to our case, it wasn't relevant. As we were conferring I felt my phone buzz in my pocket, and I was relieved when I saw it was Alice getting back to me. It's 6:30 now, she probably just got out of her family party in Oakland, heading back now. I thought about asking to see her, but she's probably exhausted and would rather get some sleep.

We piled back into the car and drove back to the station, where I immediately outlined my desire to go home. It was my day off anyway, I only came in because I had to for the case. But it only got more complicated.

I got on the phone with Ellis during my car ride home, though, to talk out some details and direction. "So how drastically do you think this changes things? Is it another killer?" I asked.

"I don't know man, it could be, but think of it this way: Jamison was twenty-six years old, so he fits the age group relatively as the others. He doesn't meet the high school criteria, but what if it was something else that the killer had in common with him?" Ellis threw back at me, and I considered it.

"Right, maybe college? Instead of high school, what if the killer met them at university? In a similar manner to the others, maybe Jamison bullied them or something along those lines, and now that they're connected locally again, the killer strikes," I said, believing so.

"We'll get on that tomorrow, I'll call Sophie and tell her to get the college of this guy. We might be onto something here."

Texting and driving as I do, I shot a text to Alice as I was almost home, asking if she wanted to come over for a drink. I prefer not to drink alone, and tonight I was dying for her company. We've been getting really close the last few weeks, and I've been enjoying myself. We'll play chess or discuss political theory, or visit museums— something new every time. Her intelligence impresses me, especially as someone who is rather narcissistic.

She told me she would be down to hang for a few hours, so I stopped by her place for a bit, and she greeted me with a pleasing smile, as she always managed to do so majestically. She was tired from the family party she attended, but was still willing enough to see me. Ever so late, the night never died.

We spoke on a variety of topics, the usual small talk. After snacking on some pretzels we moved over to her living room and turned on the nightly game show. She informed me a little about her past life, and I gave her my best effort to pay full attention. Originally, her plan was to work at home as an accomplished author, and she showed me some of her smaller writing pieces. I was thoroughly impressed.

"What held you back?" I asked, generously concerned.

"You know, I went through a rough period in my life of isolation. These works, you see, are all dark, and grim. I got tired of it, always portraying fragments of my mysterious imagination onto the expository canvas. I hadn't anyone to help me through the time, no friends, mostly seclusion from social interaction. But now, I feel enlightened again, thanks to you. This past month, though it has gone quickly, has not disappointed. I thank you for that, you've shown me how to live again," she said in a vocal essay, flattering me. I did not know I had made such a great impact on her.

"Awe, you've helped me too! I kind of lost myself for a bit, you know? But now I'm starting to regain that confidence that I once had," I said awkwardly, trying to let her know I felt similarly in my own right. Anyways, I went on to explain my initial intentions before deciding on police work.

"I also changed my career path, at first it was nothing to do with law enforcement. Rather, I aspired to enter into the athletic world in one way or another. At the end of high school, part of me wanted to continue my running career in hopes to make it to the Olympics, but I knew there was no way I would be able to maintain that focus that I had for my senior year," I began.

"I understand. I, too, was fairly unmotivated in high school. Partly what led to my writing's iniquity."

"Right, it was a hard time. So I settled on striving to be an athletic trainer, but that soon fell apart. I would always doze off in my classes, especially in one on fitness. It explained the key seven points of athleticism; strength, coordination, stamina, speed, flexibility, agility, and mentality," I started, and realized quickly that I was going off on tangents, so I strayed back on course. "Anyways, pardon me-"

"No, go ahead. It seemed to interest you. Let's talk about it," she interrupted, and I cherished it. There was something about her, in times like this, that really stood out to me. It was a sense of compassion, really, where she was genuinely affected by my own relish, a quality I had grown unfamiliar with.

We talked for some time about the spectrum of sports, oddly enough, and I learned that she played volleyball in high school. It shocked me, despite her talents, as she seemed to me extremely introverted. I never thought sports would be in her realm of activity.

The night went on, as it did, and we kept drinking. After we finished the bottle I purchased earlier in the day, she went to her cabinet to get another drink. We joked about stories, talked about our days, the usual coupled things. I could tell her attentiveness was slipping away, leaving me little incentive to stay awake. My deficiency of motivation spurred on. As the time passed by, I stopped caring about what repercussions I would have to face the following day. What did it matter if I stayed up enjoying myself tonight? It would be worth it.

I peered over at my watch and saw that it read 2:00 am before chucking it across the room onto the couch opposite our position. The night was beginning to die down, and we were probable to fall asleep in each other's arms, chatting away about whatever. She was explaining to me some story of a man she met but had to go away earlier in the day. I struggled to comprehend what she was saying, I'll have to ask her again sometime. I fell asleep with a terrible headache pounding the back of my skull and the underlying hope that my mentally-engrained alarm would wake me up.

. . .

Wow, this feels familiar. I rushed into the offices of the police station, trying to appear at least slightly prepared for the day. My efforts were to essentially no success, and I received a surplus of dirty looks from my colleagues. Oh well.

"Apologies for my tardiness, what's the plan today?" I asked, trying to tidy myself up, while looking in the general direction of Ellis and Amber, who has returned. "Well?"

We exchanged ideas, and I made it a point to share what Ellis and I had discussed the night before, with regards to looking at the college. Of course, if we decided to pursue this matter, it would complicate the issue greatly, but it may be required to make any progress. All this case has done is complicate everything—every aspect of my career. I really did wish that this case would be solved.

It made less sense to me the more I thought about it. We had such little evidence on this case, I was considering requesting assistance from higher grades of law. And then I ruled out possible avenues of action. *What can we do?* Clearly, the intelligence of this killer is beyond that of anything we have seen before. My head continued to pound.

I need something! A direction. We just have to work harder and hope for a slip up. This criminal mind appears professional, but there has to be some weakness in their game. They have to make a mistake at some point. Thumbing through the files on my desk, an idea popped into my mind, and I shouted for Ellis.

"What if we check surveillance and street cams from everywhere in the area? It might be hard to get access to them, but they might be able to have something show up," I proposed. Honestly, it was nice to have a partner who was willing to listen to ideas. It allowed me to bounce ideas off of him whenever I needed, and he'd always give me feedback. I respected it and tried to mirror it.

"I like it, I'll get on it with Amber," he agreed and went off. It gave me some time to think about the case, and in doing so, I decided to head out for the scene of the most recent crime on my own. I was always confident in my instincts, and I trust them now more than ever.

I got to the scene; it was just like before—minus the body. Here, I am to let my mind go to work. I recall, certainly, that the body was in a position like it was thrown onto the ground, though that wasn't the cause of death. Clean incisions had been made, which provided the blood stains on the ground. I scanned the area.

There. I looked up and saw a ledge where Jamison could have possibly been thrown off. It seemed impossible to get up to there from the spot I'm at now; the killer must have taken a different route. A different entry to the corridor. Thankfully, I was able to conceive how they got up there and made my way up similarly.

This always bothered me, things like these. Notice how I'm able to utilize my instinct and creativity to work through problems like these. This isn't allowed in traditional, standardized environments. I hate it. It coincides with my lackluster academic achievements in school. I never got inspired nor intrigued by some textbook curriculums. I hated it.

These institutions are designed to breed the highest GPAs and the most prolific students based on the restrictions they confine them to. Intelligence isn't the ability to study flash cards on vocabulary terms for hours on end to ace the quiz, no. Intelligence is being able to take the knowledge taught to them, and those students utilizing it to solve problems based on the subjects. Thinking for themselves, not memorization and choosing the right classes to take.

This always bothered me—it's why I never tried. I didn't care about learning systemic formulas and useless mathematical knowledge; it never mattered to me. What good was my ability to think "outside of the box" with set limitations on how I should think anyway? I could've done great in high school, I could've been first, but I chose not to be. I didn't want it. The achievement held no value to me.

See, what the world needs is creativity. Everything is so repetitive and unimaginative. This uncanny ability I have to think unusually, I have never been able to put it to use because of pointless boundaries placed around me. I don't want to follow rules when given a problem, I don't want to solve it this way or that way. Let me solve it my way, I can find the most efficient method, let me do it. At least, that's how I always thought.

I may seem quite shallow, at this point, and that I think too highly of myself. The fact is, that I do know my talents, and how little I have capitalized on them. I understand what I am capable of doing and where it is socially appropriate to do so, but I never mean to brag about them. It is not my intention to come across as condescending, as I truly believe I am inferior to most. My lack of control over my emotions is my downfall; I let them get the best of me and my judgment sometimes. They appeal to me too heavily, and I often let them control me. *How inexperienced my mind truly is.*

But anyway, as it pertains to my current situation, educational establishments never earned my respect. They're just money-hungry, corrupt organizations that feed societally-accepted information into students starving for their diplomas. Everything in the world is so centered around the idea of prestige, and where the most well-respected colleges are, and conversely, those colleges charge the most. What good is it to jack up the prices on these schools, so that less people can attend them without worry? Without student loans? Why is everything so money-driven, can't people get fair education without having to be limited by their financial situation? Especially, since many teenagers seeking collegiate experience aren't in full control of those situations? It disgusts me. This is relevant to the killer getting on top of the building, surely.

I climbed up the rigid, fragile staircase along the side of the building to reach the top. It was built next to many other buildings, which probably allows the killer easy escape routes. Now that I'm atop here, I just have to search for a lead. Where could they have gone? I let out a howl and verbally mustered "Who is it?", not expecting a response. The chilling breeze opened the realm of tranquility, and allowed me to clear my mind. I focused on the landscape, its environment, how one move can lead into another. I let my true detective nature take over.

I ran across the top of the ledge toward another building where there was a window conveniently placed to latch onto. Next to this window sill was the roof of another building that led farther down the block. I started my jump as soon as I got to the end of the building I was currently on and landed perfectly on the sill, so as not to slip, and made my way through the top of the other building.

I could smell the humidity and petrichor as thunder viciously roared over the horizon. The occasional strike of lightning intrigued me, and soon, water began to pelt the Earth from a distance, inching towards me as I approached it.

As I maneuvered around the building, scanning for escape routes, I noticed equipment on the floor. It had blood still on it, *this could be it*. I picked it up and placed it inside of the plastic bag I luckily remembered to bring and ensured that I had the evidence safely concealed in my pocket. *This could be the breakthrough in this case.*

I've never killed someone on duty, and for a moment, I was stuck in mental paralysis as the rain began to fall harder. *What if it comes down to my life or theirs?* I thought and worried precautiously. I don't know if I have the guts to do it—to take a life—whether it's necessary or not.

I snapped out of the trance and phoned back to the station for the autopsy report on our latest victim. If there was a point of insertion still from the needle, it would prove this was used in the killing, likely to tranquilize him. A compelling lead if it works out in our favor. Now, as detectives often know, the waiting game is to be played. Evidence samples and correct match-ups on loose items found at the scene of a crime to pinpoint a suspect. Often times, what interests me most, are challenge. An unknown element, no definitive answer until the evidence is conclusive enough. *The thrill of mystery.*

How easily my mind begins to trail, I hadn't made it forty-five seconds in the car without thinking about something abstract. This hour's topic happened to be what I would do if I found the killer. I mean, of course, instinct would be arrest, as taught by police duties. But something about their sinful résumé stood out to me as I played through hypothetical scenarios. *What if I did muster the courage to kill them? That makes no better than they are...*

I've always thought of myself as a person that abides by the law. My high school days were not that much of a different story, it was just my presence nearby illegal activity, not my actual involvement. And ever since my historic failures in distance running I made it my goal to stick to my craft. Inspired by the drawbacks of my indolent character, I signed a treaty with myself under the conditions that I would never slack on my loyalty to the law. No cutting corners, no taking an easier method that may skim over one or two lines of the rule book just to make ends meet. Things need to be done the right way, or else the entire police force sees and thinks identically, throwing San Francisco into a time machine to 1920s America.

Comfortably, I dismissed the idea from my trackless train of thought. I would never break the law or act solely out of emotion. I've always had a ready grip on my judgment, and I've rarely lashed out in an act of chaos. Those closest to me know my typically reserved spirit is one of my most redeeming qualities.

If the dire situation were to come down to my life or theirs, however, I would have to make a true judgment call. Not out of emotional impulse, rather lawful practicality. Hopefully, that does not come.

While I may appear timid with respect to this case and its undiscovered details, I have often dreamt of participating in a decade-defining investigation. I always wondered if current technology had been introduced to the helter-skelter police teams of the Victorian era of England, would Jack the Ripper have been caught? Surely, the "investigation" performed by the officials of the time had no real leads or evidence (and no way of processing it had they come across any). The trials of imagination can provide ludicrous experiments, if only there were more creative people in the world. It is truly a gift.

This case is shaping up to be decade-defining in its own regard, as well. Four murders and very little, if any, concrete evidence to go on, especially as I just received word that there is no apparent entry mark of the tip of a needle, but that is not to say there is none at all. Deeper examinations have yet to be made, they are only on the beginning layers of inspection. It is common knowledge that finding a sure-fire lead won't be feasible, but it is possible, with one's heart in the right place and a cleared mind. Focus is it all.

The people of the station ordinarily continued their daily business when I arrived. No abnormal greeting upon my return, but I am determined to change that. I want to have a case claimed as historic, landmark. Something I can say I did and solved, to amplify my legacy. Something to look back on, and I believe this is it. *No more lives can be lost.* The thought bounced itself around the interior walls of my skull. My greatness cannot come at the expense of others' lives, I will not let that change.

It has been some time since Alice and I last planned an eventful day together. Recent upbringings in the case mixed with genuine fatigue has not allotted very much time for leisure. I want to change that, however; I feel that I owe it to her.

I feel as if we've actually started dating, and I'd like to continue that trend. It would have to be *us* though, not some typical dine-in. Something exciting, adventurous. That's what I've found to love in life: the thrill. I don't know whether it's my poor judgment or my quest for a good time, but whatever surges my adrenaline levels makes me come alive.

Anyways, enough about me. I want to plan something special, but there's many risks and complications that are packaged with extravagant events. For instance, what if she gets scared? *No, she's more fearless than me.* What if she simply doesn't want to? These questions wedged themselves inside my brain, and refused to move. My mind trails off so easily—I'm supposed to be working. Oh well, she's more important.

I've got it! I have a motorcycle tucked away in my storage unit. Surely, I can figure out how to ride it again, it's only been a few years; I used to take it out all the time. She would love it! We'll take it on a night time cruise, right away! I've just got to get some gas and it will be a blast. I've only got a few more hours in this box, yet the day couldn't possibly drag on any slower.

Unexpectedly, the methodology of this killer has proven to be the highlight of the case and, quite frankly, my career. I studied multiple styles of murder at university but nothing to this degree of precision. Each strike has been carried out in a well thought-out, attentive matter. There has been very little room for error on our side as this killer has worked to near perfection. *How could they be so efficient? Obviously they would need some assistance, but at the same time, working alone may be easier. Less responsibility.*

I looked through files of previously solved murders from before my job began, trying to follow the footsteps of other detectives before me who solved cases like this. The legal process obstructs things, often times, but with this case, I doubt that it would serve any great purpose with its absence.

I've found, after twenty-four years of living with myself, that I often need a confidence booster, a pep talk, something of the sort. A spark plug to get me refocused and to compartmentalize any loose doubts hanging about in my mind to where I can operate with surefire accuracy. Right now is one of those moments.

A few hours of studying passed and I tossed up the day to another dreary day in the office. Nothing spectacular happened apart from my discovery. I know what I have to do to refocus: it's about trusting myself.

I'm the one who studied law, that of the rulebooks and preceding enforcers of it. I know my way around the game, and certainly this criminal will screw up. The perfect crimes remain perfect forever. *I'm going to solve this case.*

I texted Alice and asked what she was up to. Here's where I feel I may have messed up, though. It's always been a debate in my mind on who I really am. See, I've never been able to thoroughly or definitively answer the question. Of course, I'm Theodore Hawkins, a detective for the San Francisco Police Department, but as every thoughtful human being knows, that isn't what defines a person.

If life were limited to occupation and a name, I would sure not want to be alive. If everyone's purpose was not to fulfill their own destinies and aspirations, then is there really a purpose at all? What good would enslaving yourself do with no reward in the end?

I've always had this image of myself; it's an image that is seen from the likes of everyone I have ever met. Whenever I have an interaction with someone, that image alters ever so slightly. It may be noticeable, or it may be inconsequential but a change occurs. It isn't simply one image either—it's many.

There is an image of me in the mind of everyone who has ever met me, whether it was a friendly interaction at the neighborhood bike shop from seventh grade or if it's Alice, whom I interact with daily. They are all images that I can try my best to change, if inclined, but ultimately have no control over.

The basis of this discussion is really my desire to be seen as perfect. I often mask it as chivalry, this innate greed. Of course, I love to be of assistance to anyone in need. I really have valued other people's time over mine, always thinking *I'll make it up later* when it comes to myself. And so, I always offer a helping hand. At the same time, though, I don't want my personal accomplishments and talents to go unnoticed. But I also try not to flaunt them, commonly sliding reference to them into conversation.

Anyways, this gives me the tendency to overthink things: It will be three in the morning, I'm laying in my bed with all three bedroom fans on and a bottle of chilled water beside me, and I'll be hyperventilating to the reenactment of something that happened seven months ago to a person I haven't seen since. Yeah, it's this level of a meltdown.

I've even tried proving my worth to you with irrelevant flashbacks to my teenage running days. Those have no importance to my life anymore, other than the fact that I can say I won state. What's it matter now? All I know is I have the talent.

This is where I may have messed it up with Alice. Come to think of it, I haven't had much of a conversation with her since we fell drunkenly asleep last night after my rather one sided discussion. Our one sided discussion, I mean.

In trying to portray my perfection, I may have cornered myself into a trap I tried desperately to avoid. It's too difficult and, quite honestly, impossible to steer the conversation away from me. I try, I really do, to reflect questions back to her when we're talking, but the underlying narcissism beneath all of the charisma wields all power. I texted her a fragile request to pick her up, deeming it respectable not to bombard her with my delusions. And patiently and nervously, I waited for a response. Tense, the heat inside of the car began to intensify as I awaited the signal of the notorious three dots in the iMessage console.

Sure, I'm ready whenever. It cleared up any fear I had for the moment, but I was not in the clear yet. We still had to talk it through, and I owed her an apology. I took off in my car and arrived at her home pretty quickly, eager to express my reflection.

She opened the door and greeted me with the same smile I always enjoy seeing her give. I'm not sure if I can explain it through words; I suppose only the eyes of those who witness it will understand. It was reassuring to say the least. The adrenaline quickly wore off, and my heartbeat slowed from its rapidity. She could tell I was nervous, yet I'm unsure if she knew the origin of my unease.

Immediately after shutting the door, she lunged at me and wrapped her arms around my torso, and I planted my hands on her upper back, with equal tightness. As a younger individual, *here I go again*, I always had a way with flirtation. I don't mean to brag at all, in fact, I was a bit hoppy when it came to women. Bouncing from one to the next, enjoying the rush of the sex too much. I never had the time or the patience to settle down in a long-lasting relationship with a girl. It wasn't my style as an amateur idiot. Yes, I was *that* kid. Being *that* kid led me to do some pretty uncalled-for things, which shouldn't be too hard to guess what those things were. But these adventures I would go on with girls at a younger age, cruising through town at night until the cops told us not to, didn't teach me anything. That's why I regret being the playboy of the school; I learned nothing about how relationships work. Gone off to college, I focused on my studies en route to my career, so I didn't have time for a social life. Standing here now, I'm quite inexperienced.

Throughout my scramble of charged emotions, one that emerged as a significant factor was worry: I don't know what I'm thinking. All that was going through my head was if she's mad at me, she's vulnerable. I'm powerless. What if someone else eyeing her comes along and tries to take advantage, and she falls hypnotically interested with them, disregarding my existence? How selfish and rude of me to question her loyalty. I never learned these things because no one ever told me no. I did it, so of course other people have to view it as acceptable, right? Hysterical in her arms, I began to cry, remembering all of these doubtful thoughts I had in mind. I'd never been a boyfriend before, I'm still learning how to be. *How can one love when they don't have the right equipment?* I thought heartlessly.

Yet, I do love her. I know it's early—it's been about a month: It hasn't really evolved into anything incredible yet; we aren't staying at one house *every* night, but I love her. It's my first real relationship, but I hope it to be my only. How she can see past my complexities, insecurities, mental conflicts, and all of it, to my intentions. I don't know how she does it, I can't even see through it. I snapped out of it and told her, straightforward.

"I love you," I said proudly in my head and then softly in voice.

"I love you too," she said back in a courageous whisper. *How did I get so lucky?*

The next session, I'll skip. But the night was glorious. We talked briefly about my original intention of meeting her, but she brushed it off as me overthinking things. She did so in such a calming manner that it amazed me upon the first listen. I swear it, I had to replay it in my head.

"You stress yourself out too much, silly boy, have you ever thought that that may be what I like about you?" I had never been approached with this sort of digestion to my arrogance. I didn't think it real. Nevertheless, I was jaw-dropped in front of her, and she just laughed at my disbelief. I quickly invested some time into explaining my idea of riding the motorcycle while I still had her captivated. She warmed up to the idea rather easily, and we were soon off to the storage lockers to retrieve the vehicle.

Just like that, she fixed my suspicions and introduced me to a night of pleasure. *I don't think women are usually like this, I think I just found the perfect one in the batch*. We sped over to the lockers, and I fetched my key from the center console of my car and dashed over to the unit with her following closely behind me. We're so excited, it's like we're little kids again.

Luckily, we remembered to fill a gas can on the way here, or else we'd have to run back out. We filled up the small tank of the motorcycle and set off for our journey. It was quite luxurious as we paraded through the streets of San Francisco and Oakland alike, and we finished on the Northside of San Francisco for our final tour. Riding across the Golden Gate Bridge had to be one of the most remarkable experiences of my life. It was as blissful and serene as it was romantic. I couldn't quite fathom how enjoyable it was to swerve through the high-paced lanes of the bridge with the wind tumbling onto me and gently knocking the bike around and my love strapped to the back of me with her arms around my waist, enjoying it just as much as I was as we observed the cities' skylines from afar. *This is the dream.*

We were so into the moment we didn't even make note of the time or our hunger, so by the time we got back to the storage units we both felt the same way: exhausted and ravenous. Agreeing on a hole-in-the-wall Mexican diner down the street at 9:30 just to get something in our stomachs, it felt like the joy would never end. She enjoys the ride as much as I do. It's amazing.

We'd talk about improvident and lavish vacations we'd take to places all around the globe: From the likes of Honolulu, Bora Bora, the Bahamas, Sydney in Australia, to a European tour, hitting Dublin, London, Paris, Barcelona, Rome, Istanbul, and Berlin alike. It's not just my dream, it's not just her dream, it isn't even our dream alone. It's *the* dream.

I drove her home at around half past ten, and before we exited the car, she gazed into my eyes with a marvellous scrutiny. It was impressive, her eyes glowed with a vibrant aura in the darkness of the night, and I stared at them as if they were stars shining back at me. I kissed her forehead and got out of the car to walk her to the door. Exchanging our goodbyes, I pranced back to the car with nothing but a bright smile on my face, firmly painted on by her presence. Part of me wanted to ask to stay for the night, but part of me wanted to get some genuine rest, and I knew the two did not come together.

It's a good thing this is my first relationship, really. I've always been a rather conservative spender, until now. I didn't have any motivation to go on spending sprees alone, I always wanted someone to do it with or spend the money on. Now that I'm with Alice, I'm relieved to have a decent savings from my solitary days. Unfortunately, her birthday isn't for another eight months, so I really don't have much of an excuse to spend on her.

I want to treat her so well, and I know money isn't necessarily how you treat a woman, but it certainly helps. The only catch is that she doesn't like when I spend money on her, but I enjoy it. I *want* her to have a good time, money is meaningless so long as fun is had. At least, that's how I view it.

Anyways, the night rolled over as I dozed off to the melodic backdrop of my shuffled playlist, and the harmony of my peaceful dreams.

• • •

I hate the sound of alarm clocks in the morning; I find them to just be incredibly irritating. The worst, as many can relate, is when it interrupts a good dream. The noise (so obnoxious) of the little device screaming like a banshee. *Let me finish the dream.* And of course, as all people do, I lay my head back down on the pillow for another five minutes, trying to complete whatever it was my mind was imagining as it slowly slips from my memory. No wonder people hate mornings.

I went through the usual morning routine: Launch myself out of bed so I don't procrastinate getting up, mope over to the kitchen to grudgingly get my energy juice (or coffee, rather). I chomp on a piece of buttered toast as I wait for my eggs to finish cooking, but I don't even think about it. It gets to a point where the morning is almost just another simulation of sleep; it's like I can rest while I'm getting ready because it's just muscle memory. *I guess when you're this repetitive, that happens.*

Another day in the office is another day of not getting anywhere in the case. The sample I found with the syringe will take a few weeks to match a print to someone, and the chances of it actually matching are slim to none. Especially when a killer as smart as the one we have on our hands probably used latex gloves when using it to avoid this situation potentially harming them.

There's a conference call at 11:30 today, where we're going to discuss what's been going on in town lately. To be honest, aside from your petty crimes every here and there, not much has gone down outside of this case. Our efforts have been entirely focused on finding somewhere to start in regards to this case, we're beginning to lose foresight. We've got to think of the bigger picture and realize that there are more crimes that can be prevented.

The hours passed without much of anything going on, and as one would suspect, the conference call was more of the same. In the meantime, I studied more on the detectives before me, but it's all to no use. This killer is too smart. I was telling Alice the other night about some of the names on the list, trying to see if she remembered any of them from when she went to high school, but of course, she didn't.

During the meeting we talked about plans of action, and the possibility that we might have to just give up for the time being. Not to forget about it, per se, but just focus on exterminating other crimes. Although not much happens, so we might just use our downtime for nothing. I shrugged.

Another hour went by before we got the usual call-in from the first witness. This time, the body was more gruesomely murdered and thrown by the coast of the bay. A bullet through the head of the victim, but the body was placed for others to see. I question how the killer got away with doing so and not being caught, but then again, when doesn't this killer surprise me.

Ellis and I hopped in the car; it wasn't an upbeat ride. No, it was more on the depressing side. We knew this killer was better than us, just neither of us wanted to admit it. It hurt to be defeated this many times, and it doesn't seem like the killer is going to slip up.

We got to the scene and everyone from the police force sulked their way over to the lifeless body lying at the edge of the street. It was just as the witness, who was now being questioned by one of our more comforting officers, described it. A simple headshot and nothing more. I don't even know how the killer got the body here without being noticed. And then it hit me:

I investigated the body on a first glance, and the blood was fresh. It was still glistening under the sunlight, it hadn't yet dried. *This has just been done.* I looked at the direction of the body and then behind me. The blood splattered in front of the body, meaning they were shot from behind. I sprinted to an alleyway across the street. To my surprise, there was a gun resting on the ground. I yelled out to one of the investigators, "Bag it!"

The chase is on right now, this was just committed, what probably happened is they shot the kid, saw that they were open, ditched the gun, and made a run for it. *Where did they go?* I barked at Amber on com to order a patrol of at least ten squad cars around the area of our current location. They can't be very far. I dodged a few people and random barricades as I ran through the alley, peering down corridors, hoping my instincts would flare up.

I took a right turn after passing a few lanes, but I was pretty sure I lost them. I jogged back to the scene of the crime, realizing we actually have evidence now. We still had to do a few more inspections, but we're getting somewhere right now. I searched the man's figure for a wallet and found one in his front pocket. Thomas Bailey.

Each one of these deaths hurts my morale; it seriously pains me. I find it hard to understand death in its entirety, but then again, I don't really think one can fully understand it. Death is really something intangible, at its core; it's the absence of life. If something isn't alive, then it's dead. But, what happens in death?

If there is an answer, then is death really death? Or is it just a transition of life? This topic is often widely debated from a religious perspective and refuted with findings from the scientific spectrum. People often try to steer clear from escalating arguments when it comes to one's faith, as not everyone believes in the same religion, but the question remains: If someone dies and, for example, goes to Heaven, are they really dead? Or are they just alive in an alternate dimension, outside of the realm of human comprehension or imagination. No one alive on Earth has ever seen Heaven, because it's exclusive to those who have died and those worthy of entrance. But, if death is the absence of life, how can a person's spirit experience anything if it isn't alive. This doesn't question any religion, rather jeopardizes our definition of death.

Even for someone as deeply philosophical and qualified in studies as I, this question is really unanswerable. Death, I suppose, is not to be answered by a living being. It can only be understood through experience. I could argue my theory on it for some time, but it would not prove anything, nor would it expand our nonexistent knowledge of it. Not to mention the inverse question that if we don't understand death, can we understand life?

Back at the crime scene, the crew was scavenging the region for evidence, collecting anything that may be of use. There wasn't much besides the gun. First, we have to match the bullet that killed Bailey to the gun in the alley, then match the fingerprint from the gun to someone in the database, which may take too long. Alternative options are searching gun stores in the area for a recently bought gun that matches the pistol we found, but who knows when the killer purchased the gun, if it was even bought legally. Chances are that that won't help very much.

We decided to race back to the station, eager to put the pieces together. It was about time we had a breakthrough in this case, and Ellis let me know in the car: Xavier Whitfield, another officer who often works with CSI, swabbed the gun for any additional genetic evidence to go along with the fingerprint.

"It's about damn time. I was about to give up, for real," he said to me, rolling down the windows to enjoy the heat of the day. We were riding high at the moment, almost too much for our own good. Something is better than nothing, though, and something came at the right time. Right when we were all down and out for the count, now we're back. Refocused.

We zoomed back to the station probably speeding a little. Ok, definitely speeding a little. It doesn't matter. We flew into the parking lot and threw the DNA sample in the lab as quick as we could, hopeful to match with a name on the list within the next day or two. We might have our suspect, and we'd definitely catch them on this crime, it'd just be a matter of interrogation to get him for the other crimes. The only one that may not be linked is the one person who didn't attend that high school. Speaking of that, we still have to identify this last body in the list, if it's there.

I walked over to my desk which had the list of names hidden under a massive stack of papers and rummaged through them searching for the one attached to the clipboard. Once I found it, I ripped it out from under the pile and scanned it quickly for the last name "Bailey" and found our victim's name quickly. He matched the criteria for the high school. Now once we figure out the fingerprint on the gun (assuming there is one), we should have at least part of this string of murders solved. It's all about playing the waiting game and protecting those left. The number of living names on the list is slowly dwindling, so we're offering police security to each of them to ensure their safety if the killer acts irrationally or quicker than we would expect. So far, we haven't seen two murders in the same day, but killers can be unpredictable, especially those who are hardest to catch.

— Two days pass —

Following up on the lab results, we got a match! As for the past forty-eight hours, it has been pretty cut and dry. After identifying the name on the list, I went back to work at my desk and started planning questions I would ask if the gun matched up. Ballistics matched the bullet to a Glock 17, which is what I found in the alley. After finding that out, Ellis and I went around to a few of the gun stores, asking if, to their knowledge, a Glock 17 had been purchased recently. Unfortunately, none of them remembered selling one as of late, which probably means it was bought illegally.

Questions I'd ask: *"Where were you on this night, this night and this night?"* That question might be of some use, but it's easy to lie through. We'd have to verify their alibi, which could take who knows how long. *"Do you know these people?"* I could ask and show pictures of the victims. If it invokes a response, it means there's a possible connection. We'll of course search their house, but that might be tricky too. They could know we're coming and hide everything.

Before stopping at the last gun store, I told Ellis to stop at the liquor store on the way there, I felt it was a night for celebration. A vodka type of night; Alice would probably feel the same. We stopped into the last gun shop but it was to no use, they didn't have an answer for us either.

After running around town that afternoon, I headed home and picked up Alice on the way there. She was excited to hang out but thought we ought to save the bottle until we actually made an arrest, and I stood to agree. We played card games and watched Family Feud—the typical Monday night. Next morning, I woke up with her in my arms, and as I snuck out of the room, I left her an ardent note on the dresser with a key to my place. It was her day off, and I felt it wrong to wake her, so I let her have the home to herself for the day. I trust her enough.

The coffee from home, I was beginning to like more than the one from Starbucks. A few weeks ago I made a switch to save a little money, and I actually am growing to like it more. Coffee is such a bad habit, I swear.

The day at the station was pretty mellow, and it was over right when it started. Literally meetings and staring at papers for the entire day, while we all anxiously waited for the lab results. They were what our jobs were scheduled around, and what we thought of all day. Well, everyone except for me. I was still living in the night before:

We stayed up quite late again, I have seriously got to watch how much sleep I get. It's getting seriously unhealthy. I need a rest-in day, no more of this nonsense getting six hours a night. Although, I almost want to continue. I'm addicted.

I was still tasting the drink from the night before; we decided on a few Whiskey shots to spice things up. We act so wild when we're drunk, I adore her. Always seeking a good time. Finally when the day was over, at 5:00, I raced back home, ready to throw myself on my bed and sleep.

To my surprise, when I opened the door, Alice was in my kitchen preparing dinner. She stayed at my place the entire day. I started laughing the second I walked in. Picking her up and holding her close, kissing her as the chicken began to overcook—I didn't care. It was thoughtful, making my day. How quickly a day can go from boring and overlooked to joyous.

We enjoyed chicken tacos over dinner with a side of white wine, and I asked her, very curiously, what her day consisted of. I was very meticulous upon listening, because I needed something to interest me today. Nothing at work did.

"Well, I didn't wake up until about eleven thirty, and by that time I felt like having lunch. I crawled into your kitchen to make a sandwich, and after that I kinda just bummed around and watched TV the whole day. Looking through the unused apps on my phone, you know. Not much. How about you?" she asked, but I almost didn't want to tell her. It might give me P.T.S.D. *I'm kidding, it wasn't that bad, but it was really boring.*

"Well, I almost slept on the job. We'll leave it at that," I joked back. Suddenly, as I took her plate, I hesitated in front of her. A thought popped into my mind, and I didn't have time to shut my mouth before it flew from my tongue's grasp. "Do you want to move in together?" I stared at her in honest disbelief that I actually said it.

A pin-drop silence filled the room, vanquishing any elephant that may have been present. To my surprise, though, her response was subtle. It was her usual response: correct. She just knew what to say.

"Of course," she just stared back at me, stunned. We were both surprised that I actually said it, and that she agreed to it so easily. We've only been together for like a month.

"Really?" I had to verify.

"Yes! I didn't even think about that but yes! I really want to. Let's do it. My place? Or your place? Or somewhere new entirely? Oh my God!" she enthusiastically exulted.

"Let's go somewhere new. We both live in apartments—let's get a condo downtown! Overlooking the city and bay, let's get somewhere on a high-level floor. Would you like that?" I shouted. I was almost hysterical, we were actually going to move in together. She wanted to, and I wanted to.

The day went on as we researched available housing in downtown Francisco. We contemplated looking in Oakland but concurred that we would both be better suited to stay in San Fran. We didn't find anything we were certain on, but there were definitely some options. Turns out, as she told me, that she had some spare money from a fund started for her as a child. She told me some background on it but asked to keep it secret, and I am a man of my word.

Now that the past two days have been accounted for, I have an arrest to make. Yes, the lab results came back from the unidentified fingerprint on the Glock 17. Vince Moreson. Double checking with the list of residents in San Francisco who attended San Francisco University High School in the same years of the yearbooks we looked through a while back, and sure enough, his name is on there. It's go time.

We charged out of the station with the blood pumping through our bodies at a rate faster than what we've experienced lately. We got lucky that the database was able to pair the sample with a name so quickly, it can sometimes take much longer. We shot across the city with our blaring sirens and flashing lights, announcing to pedestrians we were finally making use of our forces. This killer finally made a mess, and we're here to happily clean it up.

Ellis tried making small talk in the car. "This has been one hell of a ride. Thank God we got our guy."

"One hell of a ride? What ride have you been on? We didn't get a thing done until this week. We were puppets on a string of a devious criminal mastermind who happened to make a fatal error in his method. Don't mistake this for our superiority. This is an act of luck." I had to put him in his place. This was a good way to end a dark few weeks. Justice will come; it's almost divine. Things tend to lean in favor of what's right.

While we drove to the home of the killer, I studied up on his profession with a notepad and voice from Amber over the com. Your everyday worker at the San Francisco Bank on Market Street. No one would ever suspect a thing from a guy like him.

We pulled up to his house with plenty of backup and stormed up his driveway, stomping the ground with our boots each step. Handcuffs ready, Ellis rang the doorbell, gun in hand. The guy answered with a confused look on his face, trying to play it off like he didn't know what was going on. Those were the next words out of his mouth.

"Vince Moreson, you're under arrest for the murder of Thomas Bailey," I began, placing the handcuffs on him, as I read him his rights through the protocol. First response was the same as always.

"What are you talking about? I didn't kill anyone." You know, to be fair, criminals can sometimes pull off a convincing mask if they say the right things with the right facial expressions. Moreson, however, wasn't that great. Just average, I'd say.

We threw him in the back of the car and told him to shut up. A couple of officers stayed behind to look through the house for any additional evidence as we started back toward the station. Ellis and I just wanted to get this guy detained. The sooner the better, and the sooner we could start putting pieces together and interrogating him.

As we wrestled the scared punk into the holding cells at the station, there were cheers and claps around the offices. We just solved one of the most notorious chains of murders in not only San Franciscan history, but American history. That is, if they are all tied to the same killer. The real game was about to begin.

As police officers, a big part of the job is throwing the person in question off course. Making them feel uncomfortable, hoping they slip up and crack under pressure. It's why interrogations seldom go the accused's way, because we have nothing to lose, while they have everything at stake. I kicked open the door and threw files down on the table, slamming the door shut behind me as I whipped a chair around the table and banged it on the ground before sitting myself down on it emphatically. The truth is going to come out.

"So, Mr. Moreson. What connection did you have to Mr. Thomas Bailey, whose life you felt the need to take?" I opened with, feeling confident. He countered with the innocence game.

"What are you talking about? I don't even know—wait, Thomas Bailey? The kid I went to highschool with? He's dead?" he said, showing surprise.

"Cut it out, you know he's dead. What about these? Do you recall these? Victoria Parker? Joseph Walker?" I started, spreading the images of the other four victims on the table. He didn't bat an eye at anything. *Sociopath, perhaps?* I pondered my next move. It's a chess game. I decided to castle.

"Alright, you're playing this well. I'll be back," I said, calmly, and walked out of the room.

I reconciled with the rest of the team back in the conference room, as we watched the screen of Mr. Moreson, alone in the interrogation room. "What do you guys think?" I asked them all.

"I don't know, he seems pretty innocent, I'm not gonna lie," Ellis suggested, with a smug look on his face.

"I have to agree with Ellis on this one, not something I usually do," Amber chimed in charismatically.

"I don't know, do you think he was framed? He looks clueless," Lucas added, captain of our police force. Lucas Chambers was an extremely qualified individual with over twenty-five years of police work under his belt. If he's considering that the man was framed, it's definitely a possibility.

"Alright. I'm gonna try a couple more questions first. We don't want to lose our guy because of him looking innocent. Let's wait to see what the other group pulls up from his home and see if forensics happens to shoot us back any analysis information. Until then, it can't hurt to try making him crack. If he's guilty, the truth will come free. If he's innocent, he'll be fine.

When I walked back into the room, I saw the table wet from dripped tears from the man's face. He is really selling this unimpeachable portrait if it happens to be all an act. I don't know though, I've gotta stick to questioning.

"What importance does this weapon have to you?" I said, placing the plastic bag that contained the Glock 17 used in evidence in front of him. He flinched at the sight of it.

"I hate guns, why would I ever do anything with a gun? What is that?" he yelped, and that was where I really started to believe his cries. I ran through the dates of the murders, asking him what he was doing, but he was in too much emotional shock to get out a straight answer other than "I don't know!" I almost feel bad…

Regrettably, the teams at his house radioed back to us saying they didn't find anything amazing. Wrote up a search warrant for basically nothing. And just like that, the promise we thought we held slips from our grasp with the decency of this honest man. I really thought we made way. We'll keep him in custody while we interview the bank he works at and his family. A wife and two kids. Your standard husband. This dude didn't do anything.

I chose to be a good man and asked if he'd seen anyone following him in the past month or so, anyone who would try to frame him via fingerprint theft. At this point, it would have to be someone incredibly deceptive.

Ellis and I drove over to the bank where Mr. Moreson is employed, stopping for gas on the way there. Surely, they will keep good record of what hours their workers are on the job. We casually entered through the main door and requested to meet with the manager of the bank, when we were escorted to a private room with him. His name was Mr. Jenkins.

"Victor Jenkins, manager of the bank. It's a pleasure," he said, formally. I anticipate this will be an easy meeting.

I decided to do the talking. "Hello, sir. We're conducting an investigation on a series of murders that have taken place in the city for the past few weeks, and we need surveillance or hourly records of one of your employees to verify that he was not directly involved in them," I invited, hoping he would save us the hassle of getting another court order and just lending them to us.

"Of course, I can show you his time cards for the dates you need" he informed me, and we went through the dates of all of the murders. Moreson checks out—he was at work on all of the days. Even to double check, we fast-forwarded through the surveillance of each of the days—Moreson never left the building. I think it's pretty safe to say he isn't the one who committed the murders.

I hopped back into the car with Ellis and proposed a drink after work. He agreed, and as we rode back to the station, I texted Alice, saying that I was going to be a little late on picking her up because I was grabbing a drink with Ellis. She didn't mind, telling me to pick her up whenever I could. It's already 6:00, so we're probably just going to chill for a little bit and fall asleep once I do pick her up.

We strolled into the bar and took a lousy seat at the countertop, ordering some cheap beer on tap. "Well, today was a bad day," I started.

"Yeah, it really was. It shouldn't have been. And I feel pretty damn bad about ruining that guy's day too," he testified, and I heard.

"On to the next one. We'll just have to hope for a real lead to pop up," I said, proposing a toast.

"Hey, so how are things with you and Alice, anyway? Ain't talked about her in a while, man," he queried. I was rather relieved he brought up the topic and not me.

"Ah, very well! I was actually gonna ask for your opinion on that, or well, something of the sort," I said before he cut me off with his mocking humor.

"My opinion? You mean, like, relationship advice from me? You must be kidding," he blurted, taking a sip before letting me continue.

"We're, uhm, moving in together," I awkwardly stuttered, waiting for his hyperbolized response.

He almost choked on his drink. "Didn't you just start dating her like a month ago? What, are you getting married in two weeks and a kid in three?" he jested, but then realized I was being serious. "You're being serious? Man what are you doing?"

"I guess you'd have to feel it to believe it, bro, it's real. She's into me for me, like I can feel it. I don't know, I'm probably just riding my emotions but I'm twenty-four, what else do you really expect me to do?" I laughed and finished up my drink. We stayed a bit chatting up the bartender, or well, he stayed a bit while I inserted scattered remarks to help his chances. He and the girl left a while after I did when her shift ended, and I went to pick up Alice. She was ready (as always) when I gave her the five minute text.

When I pulled into the parking lot of her apartment complex, she ran to my car, eager to get in. I couldn't help but crack a love-heavy smile. It was sweet.

We rode the elevator up in each other's arms as I was beginning to fade away. It was a long day that ended with disappointment at work. The last thing I needed was to stay up right now. I just want to fall asleep with the woman of my dreams in my arms. That's exactly what happened. *That damn alarm clock* was the last thought that popped into my mind. Eight hours later, I remembered why.

She shut it off for me since she was closer to it in the position we fell asleep in. She rolled over and whispered to me that we should both take the day off. In all honesty, I had a little bit of a headache. Not anything I couldn't work through but certainly not pleasant. I listened to her; it'd been over a year since I took a personal day, I think I've earned it. We both made our calls, and I let Ellis know if anything major happens that I'll come in anyway. I think I just need a day off of being a cop to reset my mind after yesterday. That was a lot to experience in about five and a half hours.

"So what do you want to do?" Alice cheered at me. I thought for a second and told her that I want to take her out to breakfast. She gave a stern look at first, but then reluctantly allowed it. "You just love treating me, don't you?" she chuckled, pressing her head against my chest as she hugged me.

After going out to breakfast we decided to start going through our stuff. Throwing out, donating, or trying to sell online whatever we felt we wouldn't need/want in the new home. I had a lot to go through as I kept pretty much everything that held even the slightest bit of personal value. We started with my house because Alice said she didn't have very much she would want to throw away.

First, we have to go through this dreaded closet. There's so much stuff I've just thrown in there. I really don't want to, but I know I have to. She offered to help organize the piles of what was being thrown away and what was being kept. *She's too nice to me.*

The first box held some stuff from when I was younger, including a sketchbook. Yes, I drew. No I wasn't amazing, but I taught myself how to be alright at it over the years. The drawings weren't realistic, but they were a mixture of words and abstract designs to portray messages. I pulled it out and began to flip through the pages, stopping on one that instantly sent my mind into reminiscence. It was a page filled with clouds and I knew immediately when I drew it.

—

It was the summer after I graduated high school. I had just fallen short of the ultimate goal of a high school runner in trying to break four minutes in the mile run at state. I knew I was going to give up on running in college as I didn't have any long-term dreams with it. So, being the dumb eighteen year old kid that I was, I knew I didn't have to take that good of care of my body. So, I started hanging out with *that* crowd. You know, the ones that stay up late, gangbanging through the streets, puffing on marijuana while they scream at friendly neighbors. Yeah, that kinda group.

Through hanging out with those people, of course, I met a girl. I would probably call this the first attempt at a relationship I ever had. It was certainly the first girl I cared about for more than just sex. *Wow, I'm so shallow.* Anyways, I remember nights where we'd just stay up talking for hours. Her house was always so quiet, until we started playing music in her upstairs bedroom. Her mom didn't care at all that we kicked it in her house smoking weed, so we just kept on doing it.

We had a really good thing going, her and I, I didn't want to ruin it. It was a healthy bond, we never got mad at each other, we always had each other's backs to talk or hang out. But, she started liking me for more. I swear I only wanted to be friends, but then it started spiraling out of control.

It started with late night talks turning vividly illustrative. Almost fantasies, we'd talk about. She's hint at her true intentions here and there, and I caught on but didn't acknowledge it. Sooner or later, she made it known outright to me. My initial response was just wrong—it was terrible.

"Look, I do like you. But there's something telling me it would be a bad idea. I almost don't want to like you. I just feel like it would ruin our connection we have. I don't want this to be ruined. I really like it, but that might—" I didn't even get to finish. She told me to go home. I couldn't explain myself and my pitiful justification for ruining her.

It breaks my heart still to this day. On rainy days when I'd look through my things and I'd see these drawings, I'd remember the days where we'd stay up until 3:00 in the morning drinking and smoking, having a good time. I was such a horrible person in those days. I broke her. *I wonder if she's okay.* The things I wish I didn't do.

—

I tried not to spend too much time thinking about my past. I didn't want Alice to question it and notice my ill-prepared mess of a response I was quickly trying to think up in case she did question my hesitation when I pulled out the book. I tossed it to her and told her to put it in the throw away pile—it's time I got rid of my old self. This is a new life I'm starting at twenty-four years old.

Looking through the closet, I had a lot of stuff I didn't need. Like way too much. To the point where after calculating just the stuff we're going to sell from the closet alone, it's about $250 on a rough estimate. I get too attached to things, I think that's my biggest flaw as a human being. I can't let go.

After finishing up the closet I really didn't want to keep going. It was just so much work, so I threw myself onto the couch and shut my eyes. When Alice asked me what I was doing I told her I gave up, and she just laughed and went in my bedroom. Sparking my curiosity, I followed.

"Whatcha doing?" I asked her, tapping open the door and looking for her. Before I could realize what happened she grabbed my back and shouted something, sending me into a panicked jolt.

"Wake you up?" she asked, and I smiled. "Good, now let's get back to cleaning. You want to move in together right? These things ain't gonna go through themselves!" she exclaimed, in a proud manner. I couldn't help but smile at her exaggerated productivity. How independent.

It only took about six hours to go through the rest of the house. While I did keep a lot of things, most of it was just books, high school medals and awards, and other random valuables I'm interested in keeping. It didn't take long to package it all into boxes, and we were done with it rather quickly.

Now, it's time to actually look for homes we're going to want. Of course, we have to see it in person, so the plan is to view them in person today with the rest of the day, and if we find one we like a lot pretty quickly, we can finish up going through Alice's things.

We surveyed a few condos near the police station and in other parts of the city, evaluating our options based on what we thought of them, and agreed to keep looking. It was nice that we had such open communication about these things, it helped us to get along very well. We were making decisions based on what both of us wanted, not just one or the other. It allowed things to go quite smoothly.

Our second to last condo we're looking at was in downtown San Francisco; it had a really nice view of the bay, the bridge, Alcatraz island—it was phenomenal. I loved it: a 36th floor condo, second from the top. We walked in, being shown around, and our eyes marvelled alike at the luxury. I couldn't believe how beautiful it was. It called to us instantly. The most monumental piece of it was the furniture: black and white, modern theme. It was sleek.

Three bookshelves framed the back wall of the living room, and upon seeing that we both knew this home was meant for us. It fits us almost perfectly. We knew we didn't need to see anymore.

When we got to her home to start going through her stuff, I came across the realization that we never enjoyed the bottle of vodka we planned to. Yesterday evening, I was so exhausted and I already had a drink with Ellis, it completely slipped from my mind. Truth be told I forgot I even had it. I ran back to my place to grab it, while Alice started on her closet as I did.

Quickly the night became a drinking celebration of us finding a place together. I've spent a lot of money on alcohol lately, maybe I should tone it down a bit. Anyways, we had a scandalous night of watching her telly box. We go through whole bottles with each night, we need more self control. *Or do we?* Yes, we do. *Maybe it's what keeps the fire burning between us, holding nothing back.* No we don't.

The night drifted on, and eventually we languished into a snooze. While we were babbling about she started telling me these dark stories. I didn't make much sense of it, as I had most of the bottle of vodka, if I'm being honest. After a few minutes of storytelling she began to sob uncontrollably. I didn't know what to make of it. I hardly even understood what she was saying. She was telling me that she killed a man, and that she dropped a gun as she sprinted through a backstreet. She had to pin it on someone else for her own safety, and then for mine. It confused me, I wasn't all there, and I found it hard to believe. I was seconds from passing out when she informed me of this event, so I had no recollection of it when morning came. My hearing of that anecdote is limited to her knowledge only.

I had no work tomorrow but she did, so I would probably repeat what happened with her the other morning, waking up in her house alone.

Sure enough, I did, to the backdrop of a stormy day playing through her speakers as I peered over her dressed and read aloud the heartfelt note she left for me before she went off to work for the day.

Surely it was one of the most boring days in my life. When not working, I really don't know what to do if I'm not with Alice. She's become the entirety of my life, I simply am lost without her. She was preoccupied at work all day, probably catching up on the work she missed yesterday, so I had no idea what to do. I thought about going into work even though it was my day off, but my mind favored in the direction of napping and oversleeping.

So the day lugged on and yeah, my life is really boring without Alice. How did I even live with myself? What did I do? I'm not entirely sure. I know that today, however, I'm going to read a bit more on the book I've been putting off. It's been a while since I had spare time to myself. The last time I was going to read this book, I got called in for one of the murders. Now, I finally have time to indulge in it, and I plan to without any distractions.

That's the extent of what happened today. When Alice got back to her home, she wasn't surprised to see me there. I was happy to be preparing dinner for her as she did for me, and she threw herself into my arms as I was preparing a pasta meal. It was adorable.

"How was your day, lovie?" I asked her, preparing for an unusual response.

"It was, well, a day. Not very exciting but very busy, you know? I'm a bit worn out. After dinner, why don't we take a nap, what do you say?" she offered, but I was a bit reluctant. I had a lot of energy that I didn't expend today.

"We'll see," I said, smiling at her as I set the table and made our plates, feeling good about the dinner I cooked. We sat down and ate it without usual nighttime chatter. I watched out of the window as the winds blew and used it to spark conversation. "It's nice living in San Francisco, isn't it? No worries about cold weather," I commented. I'm most definitely not a cold nor winter person. The blood in my veins freezes, and I shiver with disgust anytime the temperature dips below thirty.

"Yes it is. I've lived here for most of my life, but when I went away to Massachusetts the winters there were brutal. I really want to stay in warm areas for the rest of my life. It's so much better." We agree on so much. She even wants to live in Hawaii, which is my dream location.

Another eventful night that went similarly to the rest of them: talking, games, the usual. I'm realizing now how little friends I have, not that I had very many before. I at least had a few friends from college and high school who I would keep in touch with, but those connections have since faded. With Alice taking up so much of my time, I haven't even had time to text the few friends that I still remembered from my time in law school and college. *Compromises of relationships, I suppose.*

The next day, Saturday, went by and it was more of the same. A pretty uneventful day, if I'm being honest. It annoys me when I can't spend time with her, it really does. Time, for humans, is this finite resource that we have to carefully choose when we use it. If something gets in the way of our existing plans or intentions, our initial excuse is: "Oh, I don't have *time* for that." It's never the truth; it's never that we don't want to do it; it's that our schedules don't allow it. I'm guilty of it as well (I'm no victim of hypocrisy) but we people obsess over this unimaginable concept that controls us.

The average lifespan, at this current point in my life, is sixty eight years and four months, for males, at least. That's approximately 24,958 days, roughly 8,900 of which I have lived through. 35,939,520 minutes, and I've experienced around 12,816,000 of those minutes already. We live through, on average, less minutes than there are people in California, at the time of me explaining this thought process, of course. When put into perspective, and viewed objectively, the average lifespan is not as much time as it appears to be.

Do you know how many times I have told someone, "Can you give me a minute?" when they ask me for something or want my attention for one reason or another. I'm willing to bet thousands. That's more minutes of their time I have wasted because of my own importance and their patience. The point I'm trying to get at is essentially that time is arguably the most valuable notion that humans can perceive, but it's also the most misused. Right now, you're reading these useless facts that you've already forgotten and are glancing back at to refresh your memory. I've wasted my time calculating them at the expense of the opportunity to fulfill other aspirations I may have.

In essence, the point I'm trying to make is that time should be our key motivation for neglecting laziness, but it shouldn't cloud our thoughts. When we do go out and improve our lives or do something to brighten our future, it shouldn't be done to ensure that time is not wasted, rather it should be done to make use of the time we have. As you're reading the lines of this book, time is slipping away. Capitalize on rushes of productive ambition, don't brush them off as an unusual feeling. So many times I've felt the inclination to run the extra mile, figuratively and literally, or to study the extra thirty minutes, but dismissed it as empty thoughts. I'm positive I am not alone.

Once humans can understand that their days are limited but what they can do with their days is not, is the day progress can truly begin to take hold. It can never be too late to start something, nor can it ever be too early.

I actually have another topic I would like to reflect on while on the subject of time. While I don't fancy wasting time, and I have, since my high school days, tried to be rather cautious of it, that is not to say everything I do is productive. Time can be spent actually poisoning your body with alcohol consumption, which in theory is deteriorating the enhancement of human physiology, but still the time is utilized. I see four components, or values, of life that must be recognized: enjoyment, passion, company, and self-improvement. So long as time is spent embodied in one of these four elements, the minutes are not wasted. This is why I spend so much time with Alice—she meets all four.

Enjoyment is the basic happiness gained from the activity, vividly obvious to tell if this requirement is met. Passion is a bit deeper; for instance, one's true focus of occupation: if the time is not spent toward achieving a goal and assisting the person in reaching the goal, the time is not spent passionately. Company, is again difficult, because in my eyes, there are two types of company: company with other people, and company with oneself. Of course, time spent with other people boosts social skills and creates memories to reminisce on, as a solitary lifestyle can be detrimental to the human psyche. But spending time with yourself is equally important. It's necessary that people find out who they are, and such can only be done with introspection. Learn your temperaments, learn your limitations, and understand how your mind operates, which can only be done so with time and mastered with effort.

Lastly, deserving of its own focused piece, is self-improvement. Often times deceiving and rarely easily identifiable, time spent on oneself with the purpose of self-improvement must be dissected to its core and raw intentions to fully comprehend its beneficial integrity. A simple question, as done so many times, must be asked: Does this help or hurt us? If the answer is the latter, it is not worth the time. That's my belief, at least. Solely my own, others may choose to follow, but I will not force it upon them.

Returning back to its relationship to Alice, this is why I don't see my time as wasted with her. I see it as honorable to be able to spend it with her. I receive nothing but pure joy from her company, and she helps to open up my mind and allow me to understand it better. Even with the basic psychological knowledge that I have from prerequisite studies and self-delight, she still utilizes an elementary personality that gives room for reflection when it's needed, with respect to her and myself.

I could never loathe about a moment spent with her—she's just that remarkable to the point where I question my own worth because I truly see her as the perfect girl. Not even the perfect girl, just the perfect human being. Perfection, realistically, is unattainable, and truthfully, should not be anyone's goal. Strive for excellence, not perfection, because perfection leaves no room for improvement, eliminating one constituent of time management. But in my eyes, I cannot help but believe she was born flawless. I can't see anything in her that could be corrected or changed for the better or for my own liking. I find it hard to believe but still trust the feeling more than I should.

I spend nights overthinking things, as usual, because I feel vulnerable. Vulnerable in the sense that I'm liable to make a mistake, which would encourage her image of me to be tweaked, and changed, possibly for the worse. Once one quality of mine becomes a fallacy, the rest are exponentially easier to target. One part of my character crumbles, and inevitably, the rest of it is bound to follow. It's why I can never rest comfortably, when alone, or even in her presence, because comfort leads to unawareness, leaving room for error. With someone as perfect as her, I can't make errors. *I seriously need to relax.*

I understand it's a fixed mindset, but that's the perfectionist nature in me. I hold myself to surreal standards because I feel that I'm the only one capable of hitting them. I felt this way until I met her, and now I hold myself to standards that are even higher. Constantly driven to be good enough for her, even though she tells me to calm down. She tells me it's going to be okay. She tells me she loves me. She tells me she'll never leave me. It's not that I don't trust her. It's that I don't trust myself with this heavy of a responsibility. *I'm sorry, Alice.*

I'm probably just rambling now, but I love to. I never know who I'm talking to (though it's mostly myself.) I may be going crazy, but oh well. I like speaking my mind, it allows me to free my inner thoughts, expressing who I truly am. I was just mentioning how I get caught up in my perfectionist mentality, but I'm not the only one strung up in their own head. You see, the problem with today's generation is that everyone obsesses over being in a relationship. I'm twenty-four years old and I will proudly say that I am in my first real, serious relationship ever. It doesn't bother me.

How often is heartbreak dramatized, molded into becoming this life-ending misfortune, when it really isn't true. What happens is everyone rushes to get a boyfriend or girlfriend, in hopes that it will prove to the rest of the community around them that they are capable. Whether or not they actually have feelings for the other person is irrelevant, but the fact alone that they can say they are dating someone is enough to satisfy. It makes no sense to me, it never has. Love is something uncommonly felt, yet the phrase "I love you" is used so much.

A boy will hold a door open for a girl and ask her how her day was and instantly he likes her. No, it's called courtesy and having proper manners. Love isn't just being a nice person, that's just being a nice person. Love is the willingness to do whatever it takes, even at one's own expense, to ensure another person's happiness and safety. Staying up until two in the morning asking your significant other, making sure they stop crying. That's love, even if it isn't a significant other you're talking to.

Now that kids are in these ill-structured relationships with poorly discussed foundations, their hearts are bound to be broken. All it takes is an unwise act of infidelity and the whole relationship falls apart. It's as if an outside person, a third person, is controlling the fate of the relationship. Real love doesn't exist in the presence of a third party. If the love is mutual, there is no external affairs. There is only one person who loves another person, and another person who loves the one person back. That is the only type of loving relationship.

Of course, love can be one sided. One person can love another person without being loved back, but this type of love is rarer to find. It is often much more fragile and breakable. Eventually, sinister emotions will take over, the unloved will become angry or jealous and choose to cease communication, permanently or temporarily, forever altering the health of the relationship. *I know this too well.*

Trust is a whole other issue as it pertains to relationships and love, but that is a different discussion in its entirety. The time it would take to explain trust's place in love is immeasurable, as every relationship is built upon a different level of trust. It's incredibly intense when perused with maximum effort. *The discoveries of philosophy.*

I decided on spending the day alone, drowned in my studies, as I used to do so often. It allows me time to think about my life. I often smile alone like some idiot, thinking about my memories with Alice, the career I've built for myself, and my worldly collection of scholarship. I've always had a fascination with just being generally intelligent, not really defined to one subject excluding my occupation, but instead knowing things about a multitude of areas.

Anyways, *I say anyways a lot,* a day to myself is a bit awkward. Alice said she just felt like going home and sleeping and that she'd return to see me tomorrow, but it feels weird. We were many days strong with spending the night together; it just feels out of the ordinary to spend it alone. I fell asleep at 8:30–finally some decent rest.

A Sunday with work always felt a bit off to me. I guess it's the fact that the stereotype of the average American worker is a 9-5 job, Monday through Friday with the weekends off. Having Fridays and Saturdays off seemed a bit ahead of schedule, like it should be moved up one day. Probably just my self-diagnosed OCD that I am convinced I have.

I strolled into the station with some jazz in my walking rhythm and sat back in my chair ready to get to work for the day. I sent Alice the normal "Good morning" text, so she'll probably respond once things settle down for her. She, too, has odd days off from work. It's Tuesday and Thursday off, it's slightly unfortunate that we don't have a single day off together, forcing us to spend downtime of work days together instead of personal days. *You win some, you lose some. Or in my case, I win them all.*

A few hours passed by and she still didn't respond, and my clingy persona is starting to tingle. Nothing much, as of now, but I'm starting to worry.

Another hour flew by and I started to get genuinely scared. It's 2:00, and she hasn't said a word to me. What could she possibly be doing? I've got to see what she's up to, whether it's immoral or not, I've got to make sure she didn't get kidnapped or anything.

I searched up her cell phone on the digital tracker, expecting a reassuring answer of her work. Instead, I became frightened with the feedback that she wasn't at her work. She's located, or at least her phone is located in an old part of the city, more so on the Westside. *I have to check it out.* There's no reason for her to be there, it's far out of the way and it's nowhere near her work. Something probably happened when she prepared to go to work. Why did she have to stay home alone last night? It's got to be my fault, I should have made sure she was okay earlier. I've messed everything up. I can't lose her.

I threw the stuff off of my desk as I launched myself out of the chair and darted out of the building. I hopped in my car, forgetting to put on a seat belt for a minute as I drove extemporaneously, fumbling with my phone as I tried to pinpoint her location with directions. This is probab—definitely the most real and fearful situation I've ever been in. *What if I panic?*

This may be a true testament to my ability to work under pressure. I've habitually considered myself to be a strong-minded personage, but that is going to be tested at the highest stake right now. Pressing my foot on the gas even more, I sharply increased speed with impatient immediacy and made careful note of my surroundings. I slammed on the brakes and the car halted to a stop as I threw it in park and flung out of the driver's side door. An alleyway waited in front of me with ominous intentions, and the flood gates holding back the negative predictions burst in my mind, consuming my thoughts. I ran as fast as I could toward where the tracker indicated and hung a left where it said to.

I turned the corner, expecting to see Alice endangered, possibly tied down or strapped to a chair. The worst thought that slipped into my mind was that she was dead, lying lifeless like the first of the serial killer's victims had been just over a month ago. The darkest corners of my mind had been unlocked and were now using my mental fragility to their advantage. None of my mind's most wicked imaginations could have prepared me for what laid before my eyes. Nothing could have:

There, sixty feet in front of me, stood Alice with a knife in her hand and in front of her, a woman struggling about in a chair with a piece of duct tape over her mouth, hands zip-tied to the back of the chair. I froze as Alice turned her head and noticed me. Quickly she glanced at her pocket containing her phone and realized how I had found her.

Sweat was beading up on the back of my neck, and my hands shook with nerve as I tried to process what was going on. We had escaped the loud noise of the busy streets, leaving very little auditory obstructions between her and I. The resonance from the hands of my watch ticking sounded thunderous, with every second representative of an eternity. An entirely different lifetime, each marked with endless differences from its predecessor. I studied her facial expression for a moment, as she stood deep into my eyes. Soul-clenching was her gaze, fixated on my honesty. In an instant, she dropped the knife and took off. Running down the alley, quicker than I could have anticipated, and I followed immediately.

We crossed a street that held no cars, and I continued my chase. It had started to rain, symbolically, as I dashed after her. The drizzle was light, but felt, as droplets of water splashed on my skin and were instantly wiped off with the speed at which I was traveling. I was gaining on her. She dropped the knife, so there was no way she could harm me, at least to my knowledge. I didn't plan what I would say once I caught her, I was just focused on catching up to her.

After thirty more seconds or so, I reached striking distance and lunged my arms forward, tackling her to the ground while maintaining a tight grip around her waist. I didn't let go. I waited to catch my breath so I could speak easily, but I didn't let go. If anything, I tightened. Dirt from the ground had kicked up and stuck itself onto our sweaty faces, and tears began to drip from our unfamiliar eyes alike. I was confused. I still didn't know what was happening.

"Alice?" I questioned. I didn't even know if it was her. I couldn't think straight, it was like something was restricting my mind from fluid procedure. She stared back at me, terrified, with tears pouring from her face.

"I didn't mean to—" she began, but couldn't work up the strength to continue. I picked us both up with minimal effort from the rush of adrenaline still surging through me and pinned her to the wall across us in the alley. I stared into her eyes and, quite honestly, her spirit. I was acting on impulse. No rational thought. No logical reasoning. No thinking. Act first. Figure out what the hell I did later.

"Is it you? Are you the serial killer we've been chasing for weeks now with no evidence to go on, no idea on what direction to head in. It's been you this entire time?" I screamed at her, instilling an unthinkable fear in her. I didn't care. She said no words, only nodded. I continued my verbal march of authority.

"Is this all you met me for? That day in the coffee store, was that planned? Did you get close to me only to distract me from the case?" I kept a streamline precision in what I chose to say, careful to remain in power. *I'm in the right, she's in the wrong. I never thought this day would come.*

"Originally yes—" she started, but I didn't let her finish.

"Originally yes? What do you mean 'originally'? What changed?"

"I changed! I thought about using you and manipulating you, but I thought differently shortly after meeting you! I fell truly in love and separated my two lives apart from each other so that they could never conflict and interfere with one another. Everything I said to you, everything I felt with you, everything I did with you was all real!" she cried back to me. I couldn't tell if she was trying to play the sympathy card, but there was an earnest outcry in her voice. "I used to be a sociopath. I used to have no friends. I used to hate my life. You changed it all for me! You showed me how to love!"

"Then why did you lie? Why did you lie, Alice? Why? Why did you kill? What did you do?" I struggled to formulate complete sentences. It was merely fragments of addled horror, bits and pieces to the full sculpture implanted in my mind. What I was saying was just what escaped, what couldn't fit within the boundaries of my brain. She looked puzzled as I did.

"I didn't mean to, I tried to hide it but I was starting it a while ago as a way of getting back and I just—" again, she was cut off. She was losing the conformity of her articulation, and it was acting as a facade to her true character, her immoral character.

I kept her pinned to the wall, unable to break free, as she continued her sobbing. A few seconds went by and then I took my eyes off of her. Peering down the alley, I saw the lady Alice had imprisoned had now broken free and was actually making a phone call. *Damn it, she's calling the cops.* We have to flee. There's nothing I could do now that wouldn't appear incriminating.

We have to flee the city. Not just the city, but the state, probably the country. I have to get Alice out of here, or else she'll go to prison. I tipped her head up toward me and began to talk fast. "We have to go. Right now, Alice. You need to follow me, we're going to get in a taxi, and we're going to go to the airport, and we're going to take the first flight we can to get out of here. You need to go into hiding so that you don't get caught, and you're going to tell me everything okay?" I explained, step-by-step what we were going to do. The rain had augmented into torrential downpour, and we hiked our way through the cluttered alley, scanning the streets for the first available taxi. We found one quickly, with a bit of luck, and ordered to be taken to the San Francisco International Airport.

"Why are you doing all of this for me? You're the cop, shouldn't you be the one arresting me?" she softly questioned in the backseat of the taxi, trying to keep her voice down.

"I couldn't arrest you. I don't have the courage. Right now, I'm focused on getting you out of here without being caught," I said to her, trying to sound vocally sedative.

The driver happened to have a lead foot, and we rushed through the streets of South San Francisco and hopped out of the taxi quickly. The rain began to die down now, after our decently long drive to the airport. Convenient for our last-minute flight we would need to attend. I threw the driver all of the cash I had in my wallet, and took Alice's hand as I started for the airport's entrance. It was difficult to keep thoughts about my unoccupied police car at the scene of the crime, and what information the lady Alice had strapped to the chair was able to recall. I tried not to think about them and only focused on the task at hand: getting Alice the hell of out of San Francisco and somewhere safe, where no one would be able to find us.

We hurriedly asked for the first flight available, which happened to be Houston, Texas. It didn't matter the price right now, I could afford it. Surely it would set our plans on moving in together back a little bit, but I didn't care. We just had to go. We waited around for about thirty minutes before boarding our flight and taking off. Looking around the passengers of the flight, which was a relatively few number, nobody seemed too suspicious. Most of them were just casual travelers, leaving us to be the outliers.

I was still in uniform as I dozed off with my phone vibrating like crazy in my pocket. *Wait, phones.* I completely forgot about phones. They're gonna track me if I don't do something. I could either call and make up a story about where I went, or I could just destroy them and hope nothing comes of it. I grabbed Alice's phone and told her I needed to destroy it because the last viewed tab on my computer was a tracking of her phone. I texted Ellis and said that it was a family emergency, detailing that I wouldn't be back in town for a few days while I figured it out.

My car, after regaining rational thought process, was actually a bit out of location. They might not find it instantly, its location is a bit random. Enough thinking. I could come up with a story that would fit. I pushed it out of my mind for now, as Alice and I fell asleep on the plane ride holding each other's hands with a worried expression on our faces.

We were awoken by the sound of the flight attendant on the loudspeaker, signaling that we were soon to touch down in Houston. I had to start planning now, as well. First thing to do here was get another taxi to take us to the closest hotel where we'd get a room and settle in.

We almost jogged down the tunnel and got into the first taxi we could find. These past few hours have all been a blur, and we were both jetlagged, too. The taxi driver agreed to take us to Towneplace Suites, which was about ten minutes away with the traffic. It was an extended stay hotel, so more along the lines of a studio apartment, complete with kitchen. We got into the hotel and booked one of the only available rooms on the second floor, checked in, and sat down on the bed. She slowly walked towards me and cuddled her head into my arms and began to cry again. I've never seen her this emotional, I'm not used to it. It's taking some adjustment to have to be the sane and confident one between us, usually she assumes that position.

I stood her head up and told her to look at me so that we could talk about the day, and what on Earth has been going on for the past month. I was ready to be even more confused, but I hoped for an easier understanding. "Alice, I don't want you to leave out anything. Tell me everything from the beginning," I eased into the conversation.

"Okay, it started back when I was in high school. As you know, I'm not the most social person. I don't do too well with making friends and basic social skills. I'm a bit awkward and introverted," she commenced, which sounded familiar from her earlier attempt at an explanation, "I was often bullied in high school and it took a great toll on me. So much so that I quickly fell into depression, and all the horrors that it entailed. Inside me was a growing need for revenge, though. I graduated high school from San Francisco University High School and then went off to University of California at Berkeley for my college studies. I lied about it to you, I know, but I had to make up a story to protect myself. I'm sorry," she said and looked at her lap in disappointment.

"Love, you've lied about a ton. That's the least of my worries right now. We're in Houston. Continue the story," I calmly encouraged.

"So when I returned to San Francisco, I was finally free from all of the bullying that took place in high school and college, but I was still feeling angry at the world, quite honestly, for everything that had been done to me. I needed to get back at it somehow, and with this growing evil passion inside of me, I finally decided to let it loose. So, I started to murder the people that wronged me in my earlier days, untraceable so I would never allow the evidence to lead back to me, but once I took the first life of Victoria, I had to keep going. I had to continue killing; it was like this hunger that needed to be pleased. And so, I kept doing it, including one of my enemies from college, and then you finally caught me in the act, today. A few hours ago," she told me, the entire story. I waited a few minutes before trying a response, just taking it all in to understand its dimensions. Everything that had happened, was it all based on her true motives? Was our relationship really built on a foundation of lies and greed? Was any of it real? I had to know more.

"So you're the murderer. Why did you choose to toy with me then?" I asked, hoping to provoke her into giving an angry response. Instead, she kept her calamity. It makes it hard to tell if it's the truth with her paradoxical appearance. The line dividing calculated responses from impulsive action has been obscured. *Reality, return to me!*

"I didn't toy with you. What we have is real. Since the first day we began to talk in the coffee shop, I felt empowered with you. I liked the time we spent together. I wanted it more. I didn't want this to come crashing down on us. I wanted to keep you forever. You were my one and only, Teddy; it's been you since I met you," she said with a sweetheart touch. I didn't know if I should trust it or not.

"I see now how belittled I actually am. How meaningless I actually am," I said, cold-hearted, as I stared her in the eye.

"But you're my true love!" she screamed back, but I cut her off.

"That's all I am," She froze. I froze. I had no understanding of what I had just said. I didn't know the implications, I didn't know. For the first time, possibly ever, I didn't know what to do. I needed someone to guide me. Someone to tell me the way. This melancholy tragedy, what has she done to me? This morose indignation—I don't even know who she is anymore.

The power of love and the strength of dignity oscillate in my mind like a pendulum, intensively swinging from one side to another, the decisions challenging each other. *What do I do?*

"What have I done?" I said to myself and repeated. "What have I done?"

"I'm sorry. I know it may be impossible to forgive, but I don't want this to ruin what we have. There's more to us than this. We're unbreakable," she said to me, but those were her last words. Not "I love you" or "I will never forget you". No, it was that we're unbreakable. Not her and not I alone. Only us. Together.

I didn't even realize what had happened until it was already too late. In front of where I stood was the kitchen countertop with the knife rack firmly set in the corner next to the fridge. She got up behind me and wrapped her arms around my waist to comfort me, but I'm not sure that's what set it off. Before my mind could hold my arms back, I reached for the first knife I could grab out of the counter and sprung backward with it in hand, lunging at Alice, piercing her through her stomach. I stared down at my assassination with awe and disgust. Tears churned from both of our eyes, crying in sync as we did so often. I left the knife inside of her stomach, but it didn't matter. So far gone. She was dying, mouth open and choking on the remnants of what blood hadn't sept through her exposed skin. *My God. I'm just like her.*

It took me a few minutes to really wake up and understand that I'm now a felon. I'm no longer the average citizen. I'm no longer a cop for the San Francisco Police Department. I'm no longer *just* Theodore Hawkins. It took killing someone to become more of a person. "Simple" is no longer my basic character, I've morphed into something else. I've become a murderer.

I don't even care what happens at this point. My life has flipped completely upside down. There comes a time in everyone's life where they stand eye to eye with their true characters. A mirror reflection of themselves, except all masks and costumes are removed. It's who they really are, whether it's who they've tried to portray or who they've tried to hide. Either way, I'm now at that moment.

I stood, perplexed and puzzled, with my back arching over the lifeless body of the love of my life. Tears dripped from my face onto her as I tried to picture her still alive. I tried to picture her laughing personality with her impressive smile. That smile. I'll never forget that smile.

At this point, I owe her a piece of my mind. The silence of the room reverberated intensely, perforating my ear's familiarity with quiet. I'd become accustomed to her company, but now knowing that she's in the same room as me, but not with me, it made my heart sink. It felt as if my heart had been dislodged and was beginning to slip from position, shattering organs below it as it sunk to the bottom of my intestines. I couldn't quite make out what the feeling was; it was as if losing Alice had literally taken something out of me. Not just an emotional removal, but like a piece of me was amputated. Unfortunately, I happened to be the surgeon.

What a loss of talent, honestly. I'd never met a brighter woman in my life, and believe me, I've met many women. She just had *it*. I'm not entirely sure what *it* is, but she just had it. That ability to portray wisdom and sincerity with equal power, making me feel it. She was vividly intellectual, of the sort that I'd only seen in comics or television programs. It blew me away the first time I met her and continued to do so the closer we grew and the deeper I ventured into her character.

She would've done such great things. If she didn't get caught up in this murderous, villainous mess. She would've gone on to change the world, she had that sort of gift. She could've done whatever she put her mind to. If only those damn kids didn't torment her years ago, the thirst for revenge would have never manifested inside of her. She would have never felt the need to come out on top. To prove her worth, both to herself and to those who doubted and mocked her. Why do people do this?

What good comes from forcefully putting someone down? So what if they're a social outcast? So what if they don't think the same way as you? Why force them to struggle with this mental affliction? Who gains self esteem from others' failure? *It was their fault.*

Maybe that's the world's greatest ill. Specifically, it's the greatest ill of mankind. This lack of empathy for other people's struggles. No one has ever gone through another person's life, experienced the same hardships, saw the world from the same eyes. Who gives anyone the right to judge someone for their personality or opinion? And for those who mock people trying to better themselves—despicable. There's things in this world that I absolutely cannot stand, and that happens to be one of them. I guess I have too high of standards for such a corrupted species as human beings. My final thought on the matter: stick to yourself unless you're going to help someone else better themselves. Negativity is not something that should be erased, but it certainly should be the minority to positive vibes, unlike the world's current state of being.

I spent a few more minutes reflecting on the memories I made with her before I realized that I had to do something about the dead body in my hotel room. I dragged her to the closet and hid her in the back corner. I figured it would at least buy me a little bit of time, since I was broke in terms of escape plans. I have got to get out and go somewhere else. Where? I'm not sure. But I have to go somewhere to breathe and recover. I need to forget about Alice for a minute and just try to survive.

Not much time went by before I made up my mind. It's quite late now. With time zones shifting it's now about 10:30, so I decided to head out towards the city. I picked up a ride from a taxi shortly after leaving the hotel lobby, knowing I had no plans on returning. The taxi brought me to the inner city of Houston, where I walked along the streets.

I spent the night looking for a girl to accompany me, as the darkness was beginning to overtake my spirits. I settled on a prostitute, hidden down the street near a lamp. She was shivering, though it wasn't cold. Possibly from fear? I approached her, trying to mask the monster inside of me, hoping to come off as at least a little bit friendly. I told her I wanted her for the night, and she accepted the offer unwillingly. I had little money in my bank account, but enough for my upcoming plans. She showed me the way to a nearby hotel, where I purchased the cheapest room available. An ATM allowed me to withdraw some cash to give to her. I didn't really care too much about the amount. I handed her eight hundred-dollar bills upon entry into our room.

As soon as I climbed on top of the neatly made bed, she followed, attempting to engage in sexual contact. I stopped her, though. It wasn't what I hired her for. "I don't want you for this. No sex," I whispered to her, releasing a sigh.

"Wait, are you sure? What do you want me for then?" she inquired, looking unsure. I grabbed her by her chin, aiming her misguided eyes into my own, and thought of the right words to say, sincerely.

"Honey, I just need company. I'm a bit unsteady. I saw you alone on the street and felt you might be able to use it too," I said, meaning every word. I couldn't hold back the tears any longer. I burst into an hysterical cry and plunged my head into her lap. It was unfamiliar at first, but she rubbed the back of my head, easily, and asked if I was okay.

"What's wrong? Was it me?" she asked. She was so worried. I felt bad, honestly, it really hit my heart. This girl seems to have such an abused view of herself. Little self confidence. I've always been able to judge people pretty well, this was no different, just felt a bit more real than other times.

"It's just been a rough little patch of time. Not many things have gone my way as of late. I've lost direction. Do you do drugs, sweetheart?" I asked her, still crying in her arms. She paused for a second before uttering a response.

"It's kind of the deepest secret of mine, how did you know?"

"The needle marks on your arm. I'll bet most people don't pay attention to them since they're too busy with your body. There's other ways you can find success, and money isn't everything. Go out there and fix yourself," I demanded at the end. I tried to be inspiring but at this point, I'm really just annoyed, pissed at life, and anxious to die.

I checked my phone for the first time in several hours and noticed that I had messages from Ellis. They got the lab results from the syringe I sent in a while back, it matched up with Alice. *She made a mistake. Two, actually. Her first one associating herself with a demon like me.* They would've found out it was her anyway. He told me that he was sorry but that he was also worried that I'd done something stupid. I threw my phone across the room, scaring my companion.

She handed me the baggie from her purse, Heroin, and I told her I'd pay her for it next time I got to an ATM. I paid in cash at the rather poor hotel, so there's no way I could get tracked to here. Right now, I'm in the wind. Should be safe in here, if I'm able to last until sometime tomorrow. I fell asleep, without a care in the world, with the girl's body curled into mine, and my arms around her waist. *Please, God, not another nightmare. I've already lived one.*

We woke up and I asked her to stay for a while. I wanted company. To be honest, I enjoyed hers. She was incredibly beautiful, despite her drug use, and even though I don't know her name, she still managed to be comforting. She must have only used a few times, her face seems to be intact—flawless.

After some time went by, I decided to walk around the city, exploring an unfamiliar area. There were stores and restaurants and busy streets and sidewalks as all popular cities do, especially one growing as rapidly as Houston. I thought for a second about what life would be like being raised here instead of California. Still warm weather but not as balanced. Completely different culture and lifestyle, though.

Walking by a few less populated stores, I noticed one that really caught my eye. I had just bought a bottle of vodka from the place next to it, but I needed to get something from this other store, so I went in with the appropriate license and purchased it, taking the final hit on my bank account. I left the shop and started back for the hotel.

I technically had to check out of the room by 3:00 in the afternoon, and right now, it's only 11:00 in the morning. I'll be okay. The girl, Brittany, I found out, was waiting there as I'd expected. *Fake, but a similar feeling.* She was documenting everything that I was telling her. Life tips (so unwise)—ones that she still has time to utilize, being that she's probably under 20.

I told her she could leave the room now, but that she should really try to put the life of prostitution in the past. It didn't have a good ending. As she opened the door I grabbed her hand and pulled her closer to me, giving one last piece of advice I hope she never forgets, but hope that I do.

"As a man who has lost everything. Always bet on yourself, there's nothing to lose."

I assume the police have probably dug up Alice's body by now, as a couple of hours have passed since I woke up this morning. I went to the front desk of the hotel and asked for another day, and again, paid in cash. My funds are quickly dwindling, but it's alright. When everything else has been depleted, what's it really matter?

I now have until 3:00 the next day, which probably won't last as the police are likely to find me by then. *More time for me to wallow in dejection.* I sat down with my phone in hand and a charger I'd picked up from my short crusade of shopping. I began to type, and type I did for hours on end. Typing my life away, I concluded with this:

I never would've been able to thank her for the moments we shared and the days we let slip away at the fault of our own curiosity. It was a wild ride, adventurous to say the least. Though it lasted only around a month or so, it's still something I would never be able to forget or match in future endeavors. At least she had reason for taking lives, I took her life for none at all. She destroyed me. But at the same time, she built me up. She gave me everything. She showed me the good in everything. I regret terribly the truth that she hid this side of her. Oh, how I wish it wasn't her. The love that existed between us was real, undeniably real. I put love over duty, amor in officium. Quite possibly my most firm choice, one I do wish hadn't needed to be made. But such is life. And upon concluding this message, mine is no longer.

I pressed the heroin-loaded syringe against my skin, piercing it for the first and only time. I loaded the gun correctly as I waited for the effect of the drug to take place. And soon, the time arrived. The shot from the gun was the last sound I'd ever hear, as I fell back across the bed, phone in hand. Lifeless. To be reunited with Alice, once and for all.

Epilogue

So, this is what it's like to see everything. To know everything. To be everywhere, with infinite knowledge. Even still, as free as I am now, it is not the most sovereign state I have ever experienced. In fact, I feel restricted. Tied down by theoretical rope I cannot seem to break free from, much less understand. I want to return to the world, but I can't. I can only spectate, nothing more. I feel so powerless, though vaguely connected with Alice; it just isn't the same. It isn't the same link. It isn't the same relationship. Especially since our last memory together is me stabbing her in the gut with a knife in a hotel room two thousand miles away from where we live.

My typed-out autobiography, written in under twenty-four hours was found upon forced entry into my room. Probably from the heard gunshot, freaking out some other guests. Oh well. The first thing the police did was confiscate the cell phone, gun, and every other belonging I had to my name. After reading the last few bits of the narrative, they realized I had killed her. They, the Houston police, kept the phone tucked away as they went to investigate the other hotel.

Turns out the housekeeping of the hotel did a rather poor job, not even checking the closet when they went into the room to clean up. Alice was still stuffed away in the closet, same position I had left her in.

Both our bodies were airlifted back to San Francisco, where the police department was in pulsating shock. Most of them confused from what had been going on and detached from the entire situation. They were trying to put the pieces together, and since the Houston Police Department were the ones in possession of my phone, they kept it as evidence. I felt my record of the events was never to be released, but they partnered with a publishing company a few years later to spread it to the masses.

By this time, Ellis had continued working on as a detective, forever mourning the loss of myself, but moved on in terms of his job. Another detective, his new partner, came along to take my place. Chemistry continued to grow, absent of my charisma, but trying to return to the form it had assumed when I was there.

It's astonishing to see the changes that go on over time. Once my documentary got published, the entire station was in uproar, and compelled to read it. They all agreed it had an eerie, disturbed feeling to it. They had no idea how I truly felt. How emotionless I was, yet my thoughts raced. How broken yet in reach of the tools to mend. How lost yet directed by the map which I chose to create.

It's like I returned to my old self, looking back at it. Like I shoved that inner-me into a locked box and threw away the key, only to stumble across it embedded in the form of a woman eight years later. But, the contents of the box had grown over time and amplified their potency. They wound between the characteristics of my tortured mind and extended until they could touch the deepest and most buried pieces of my fragmented constitutional makeup. The laws I placed on myself, the social contract I signed with myself, the Locke influences, and the solemn persona rewrote it all. All of the philosophy I studied—it found a way to recode those words. *The effect she had, maybe I was exaggerating it. Impossible.*

I hope my scripture provides luminary insight into what not to do. Mentally challenged and destined to break with any quest I set off on, where not even the strongest prescriptions could fix it. I don't know if there was another solution apart from her; it's just the tragic hero in me didn't want to test the theory. No one knew about the nightmares. No one knew about the doubt. No one knew about the regret. Not even I knew about most of it. Not until I wrote it out.

I've said it before, only to myself, but nevertheless, love is that path that diverges, except each direction leads to the same outcome. I didn't know heartbreak could be so real. I didn't know a broken heart could actually be what kills me, especially since I'd never cared enough to have one severed this deeply. I thought we were inseparable. Turns out, any good thing can be ruined if I'm in its proximity. Not all love is like this, just for me, I believe. I was not built for it; it wasn't in my plan.

I only ever felt one true emotion. Now, when I can't even feel, I'm learning what the others feel like. The one arising most strongly happens to be hatred. Not at anyone else, not at the world or its conditions, only at me. I ruined everything that ever made me happy, and I killed the one person I loved. *How could anyone ever love me back?* Her undying fidelity, I admired it, I cherished it, except for her commitment to more sinister activities. Now, alone, I remain here asking myself useless questions. Although quite honestly, I may have only ever gotten full closure when alone. No one around me means no one around me to get hurt. It's just the negativity in me, the only way I could ever live with myself, to dwell in my own misery and sorrow. But I believe it's best for all. In isolation, hospitality.

The darkness would always stem the most boundless thoughts, and this moment is no different as I observe the world without me. Does anyone ever really live? Or is it just an endless search of dissatisfaction, hoping that something will change the course of their life for them? Not for me to make the call, for I never really lived. My own insecurity held me back from everything I ever wanted, and my own insanity crushed every dream I had right in front of me, I reflect.

...

Special Thanks TO:

Manny Gapio

Nick Martin

Jay Pillai

Lilly Joy

Tim Moriarty

Ryan Brogan

James Ochoa

Mark Ogarek

Leo Ruiz

Marie Hartman

13280944R00063

Made in the USA
Lexington, KY
29 October 2018